RAG AND BONE WINTER HOPE

A CHRISTMAS VICTORIAN ROMANCE

ROSIE SWAN

PUREREAD.COM

CONTENTS

PROLOGUE

The darkness was overwhelming as sixteen-year-old Charlotte Weston woke up screaming, tears streaming down her face. She was terrified and could feel something heavy pressing down on her chest. She tried to move but the weight seemed like it would crush her, and then suddenly it was all gone and she could breathe again.

"Up on your feet, Weston."

The vicious male voice brought back the terror once again. She was lying on a very thin mattress on the freezing floor and as the cold seeped through her threadbare coat, she shivered uncontrollably.

"Don't make me raise you to your feet, Weston," the voice went on and Charlie scrambled to her feet, feeling weak from lack of food and water for days now. That was the punishment for those who dared to talk back to the matron in charge of the children's section of the workhouse. Her malnourished body made everyone think she was younger than sixteen and so she hadn't been moved to the women's section of the workhouse yet.

"It seems like Weston needs another beating," a second person joined the first. "This girl is too insolent for her own good."

Charlie let her tears fall as she trembled before the two large figures. Since the small room was very dimly lit, she could barely make out the men's features. But their voices were known to her. It was the dreaded workhouse Master, Mr. Elver, and his equally frightening assistant. Her face was swollen from the slaps she'd received for refusing to let one of the male matrons in the workhouse touch her. She had fought viciously like a wild cat and broken his nose and that was how she'd ended up in this horrible room.

Six years of being punished for the slightest mistakes and she'd thought that was bad. But nothing was worse than when some of the men who were employed at the workhouse bribed their way into the girls' and women's section and harassed them. When she was a tiny girl, no one had bothered her. But now that she was growing and turning into a young woman, she was harassed no end.

"Allow me to show this delinquent what to expect for her insolence," the second person spoke. It was a low voice and filled Charlie with terror. Only known to the children as Death Angel, he was the worst of them all, and the inmates both young and old were terrified of his perversions. No one was safe from the Death Angel.

When she'd first been brought to the workhouse at the age of ten, she'd begged them not to lock her up. She'd begged her father not to leave her behind and promised to be a good girl. But he'd walked away without once glancing back, and she had cried for days.

Thinking that disobedience would get her sent away, Charlie had disobeyed every order given, and no matter how severely punished she was for it, she held on to her stubbornness. Her hope was that they would get tired of punishing her and send her home. But the more she resisted, the harsher the punishments became and it seemed like the wardens or jailors (as she thought of them in her head, for she couldn't speak the words out loud) only became more brutal and seemed to enjoy beating, humiliating and tormenting Charlie and her peers. It didn't matter that nearly every week three or four children died as a result of the punishments meted out to them. The wardens explained it to the officials who came around to investigate that it was one illness or the other.

Now that she was grown and could understand what was going on, Charlie knew that the officials were often bribed to turn the other way, and so the torment continued. Her hope for being rescued dwindled as the years came and went, and the days rolled into weeks and months. Charlie only always knew that it was Christmas again when they were served an extra bun with the watery broth that was their daily meal. Those who were lucky found a piece of hard meat in their broth. Once a year that was the special meal they got.

"Let me at her," the Death Angel was saying.

"Leave her alone," the first person said sharply. "We don't want to cause any more trouble for ourselves. As it is, you've caused me enough problems with the Parish Guardians, and I'm not going to allow you do it anymore."

"Just give me a few minutes alone in the dark with this one," he whined.

"No, and if you don't leave at once, you'll be sorry. And I warn you, stay away from this girl or you're just asking for trouble." Charlie heard the Death Angel mumbling as he moved away from the door, and she held her breath waiting for whatever would come next. Usually it was a resounding slap across the face, and she wasn't disappointed.

"Next time you scream and cause havoc, I'll slit your throat," she was informed and then the door clanged shut. Charlie sank onto the floor, shaking with fear at what might have happened had she not woken up screaming. Much as she loathed and feared the Master in equal measure, he had saved her life and virtue once again. It was a battle to preserve her virtue, but she was determined that they would have to kill her first before they snatched this from her as well.

She'd already lost her mother, the only home she'd known for ten years even though that was another nightmare on its own, and her freedom. Her childhood was slipping by. As she put her face on her raised knees and sobbed, it finally occurred to the distraught girl that whatever reason she had endured the abuse so long for would never happen. She would never be free, and this horrible life would never end. Her tormentors would never cease from their cruelty, her father would never return to take her back home, and no one would ever help her. She was unlovely and unloved, as one of the wardens liked to bark at her. Or else she wouldn't have been brought to the workhouse by her own father.

Charlie wiped her face as something like a stone settled within her heart. If this is what the rest of her life was going to be like, then she would stop feeling anything at all. No more sadness, and no more happiness either. She would merely exist and let the days go by until one day her cold and lifeless body would be discovered on the freezing floor of this terrible Leeds workhouse.

END OF AN ERA

Two Years Later

"I can't say I'm sorry to see this one leave," the thin voice spoke in a whisper that carried to where Charlotte Weston was standing in readiness to leave the workhouse forever. This had been her home for a decade shy two years and even though all she had known was pain and humiliation, she felt that she would somehow miss the place. This awful place was where she had grown up.

"Charlotte Weston," the woman calling the roll call snarled at her. Charlie merely looked at her with eyes that were cold and flat. And as the woman was to remark to one of her colleagues later, it was like looking into the eyes of a soulless person. Charlie Weston as they had all taken to calling her, had no soul.

"Do you want me to send you back inside and stop you from leaving?" The woman snapped but Charlie stood there wordlessly looking at her. Charlie knew that there was no way the woman would carry out her threat. She was finally free, and it was happening just two days before her eighteenth birthday. Everyone in the workhouse knew that once an able-bodied person turned eighteen, they had to leave this particular workhouse that had been especially built to take in children under the ages of eighteen and their mothers. Some children chose to stay on even after turning eighteen and so bribed the wardens to lie about their ages. But not Charlie! Even though she had nowhere to go, she wanted out of this place because she felt like she was about to lose her whole soul. And besides that, she had a mission to fulfil, one of vengeance and there was no way she could do it while in this place. So she tightened her lips and fixed her eyes on the warden. The woman seemed to get flustered at Charlie's unnerving stare and then flung a small envelope at Charlie's feet. "Those are your dues for the eight years you've worked in this place," she said.

Charlie bent down to retrieve the envelope, but she didn't bother opening it to check what was inside it. Her main desire was to step out of the workhouse and experience sunshine once again. And then her plans to get even with those who had hurt her would begin.

"Aren't you going to open the envelope and confirm your wages?"

"Whatever for?" Charlie actually sounded surprised. "If you say all my wages are in here, then I believe you for I have no cause to doubt your word, Ma'am." She gave the woman a tight smile. "In any case, I never expected to walk out of here with a single penny so," she shrugged, "whatever is in here is actually something of a bonus."

The woman shook her head slowly, not knowing what to make of the eighteen-year-old, very beautiful woman with very cold eyes and an equally icy demeanour.

"I better get going now," Charlie picked up all her worldly possessions which consisted of a small bag with the two old dresses that she owned. She had discarded her ugly sackcloth uniform when it was announced that she was being set free. When she got to the door, she turned around. "Mrs. Elver?"

"What now?" The woman snapped.

"You are one of the good ones, don't let this place change you too much." And the woman glimpsed the first real smile that had ever crossed Charlie's lips, at least in her sight. The woman saw the sweet and innocent person behind it, before the shutters fell again and she was once again faced with the girl's coldness. "You saved my life, and one day you will be rewarded for your kindness. Stay well." And with those words she walked out of the large building, to the single gate and nodded at the porter who merely grunted as he opened the door. Charlie stepped out of the place that had been home to her for eight years and felt that she could finally breathe. Eight years of torment, torture, humiliation and shame; and she had come out alive. Just barely! Though she wasn't the only one being released out into the world on this particular day, she had no interest in getting into conversation with anyone. The faster she got away from this place, the sooner her life would move on.

It was true that Mrs. Elver, who was one of the matrons, had saved her life when she'd first come to the workhouse. After a sever flogging by the master, Charlie had lost consciousness and lay in a pool of her own blood. It was Mrs. Elver who had come in and stopped the man from continuing with the punishment, wrapped the half-conscious girl in her shawl and carried her to the infirmary where she nursed her for days. Even though Charlie eventually found out that the woman had done it because she feared the repercussions of an inmate's death, the young woman was grateful for her intervention. It was also Mrs. Elver who had told her that her father had signed her freedom away and declared that she could only be released on her eighteenth birthday.

As Charlie walked to the end of the road, she turned around and looked back at the large workhouse that was more of a prison than anything else. Thick, dark clouds hang over it, signifying the coming rain, but it reminded Charlie of a haunted house. And Charlie felt like the place was indeed haunted by the ghosts of all the little children who had suffered and perished behind those thick walls. Hopelessness and despair were the norm and some just gave up, lay down and wished for death. Charlie had fought hard, and she felt weary. It seemed like a dream that she was finally free. No one would ever imprison her again.

"Never again," she vowed to herself. But then she smiled as she walked away for the last time. Leeds wasn't the place she was going to continue living in because her family home was just a few miles away. It reminded her of when her father had brought her here, unconscious, and left her at the mercy of the master and matrons whose sole mission in life had seemed to be the breaking of those in their charge. And they would have broken her, but for Ragland. On the very day that her father had dumped her at the workhouse in Leeds, twelve-year-old Ragland had come in with his ailing mother and twin infant brothers. Fallen upon hard times after his father was killed in a coal mine explosion, the family had nowhere else to go and ended up in the workhouse. Sadly, his mother and siblings had died just weeks later from dysentery, and he was left all alone.

Charlie had never understood how it was that Ragland had ended up in the girls' section of the workhouse for the first two years. They had been friends for nearly two months before she discovered that he was a boy. He'd sworn her to secrecy but eventually his deepening voice had made the matrons suspicious. That discovery had led to him being moved to the boys' dormitory, but it hadn't stopped their friendship from growing.

Even though their quarters were separate and there was a strict code that boys and girls should never be found together, Ragland had always found a way to sneak into Charlie's dormitory and bring her something to eat or even a book to read. She had no idea where he got those things from and she'd never dared to ask him. The way he was able to sneak into the women's section of the workhouse was by dressing up as a woman, and for a long time no one ever discovered his secret. He'd seemed fearless and on more than one occasion he had told Charlie that when they got out of the workhouse, he would marry her. And she had loved him with all the gentle love of a budding young girl. He was too clever to be caught and she had enjoyed their times together, building castles in the air about their new lives outside the workhouse.

"Oh Ragland," Charlie whispered. "We would be walking out of here together today," she allowed herself a brief moment of grief for her friend who had died just two summers ago after falling from one of the top windows of the warehouse in his attempt to escape from the workhouse. Charlie always suspected that Ragland had been pushed, but with no evidence she as well as everyone else had accepted the story that her best friend had accidentally fallen to his death. One junior matron had dared suggest that it was suicide, but quickly recanted her words when Charlie fixed her eyes on her and dared her to repeat that statement.

Ragland hadn't been educated at all, but he had taught her how to fight and when to retreat. He had showed her how to protect herself from the amorous advances of the male supervisors at the workhouse. His last act of kindness to her had been the stabbing of a man who had cornered Charlie and tried to force himself on her. Charlie suspected that after Ragland told her to flee, he had gotten rid of the man's body. Since she never saw that particular creature again, she suspected that he had died. No one had ever found the man's body, and that was a secret Charlie would carry with her to the grave.

Charlie also suspected that the disappearance of the man was the reason Ragland was dead. Unable to cope with the horror of what he'd done, he had changed and stopped seeking her out. A few days after the frightening incident, Ragland had told Charlie that he would be leaving the workhouse and never coming back again. She had wept and begged him not to leave her, but he'd turned his back on her and walked away. That was the last time she saw her daring friend alive.

Days later, word reached her that Ragland's broken body had been discovered by someone who had been fishing downstream. Because of the workhouse uniform he was found wearing, he'd quickly been identified and the relevant authorities informed. Rumours went around the workhouse that Ragland had tried to escape, but someone saw him and in the ensuing pursuit, he'd fallen off the top floor and plummeted to his death on the rocks below as the back of the workhouse was built above the dark and miry banks of River Aire. Like the other factories and workhouses in Leeds, this one had been built on the bank of the river where it spewed out its filth, and the stench was sickening. That was the perfect site for the factories and workhouses that were chambers of horror and no doubt meant to deter anyone from escaping once they were locked up in there.

Charlie had a mind to travel back to Wetherby and her father's estate just to show him that even though he'd left her to die in the workhouse, she had survived. But she quickly banished that thought from her mind. She knew that if she ever came across her father, stepmother and half siblings, she wouldn't be responsible for her actions, which might be maniacal. No, let them think that she had died in the workhouse because she had no desire to ever see them again. She would plan out her mode of revenge, execute it and they would be none the wiser. A sinister smile broke out on her lips as she thought about the different forms of suffering she would inflict on her family. They wouldn't know what was harming them until they were completely destroyed. It was such thoughts of vengeance that had kept her going in the eight years she'd been in the workhouse.

Charlie walked for a long time until she found herself outside the Leeds park. Winter was just ending, though the clouds were still heavy in the sky. She could see signs that signalled the beginning of spring in the plants that were breaking through the ground.

"Newness of Life," someone had once said of spring and she twisted her lips cynically. She ought to be happy that her release from the workhouse was coming at the beginning of spring when the weather would be warm. Having spent eight horrible winters in the workhouse, she welcomed the weak sunlight obscured by the heavy clouds and raised her face upward. Of course, the matrons would let them out of the workhouse for an hour each day during warm seasons as the whole place was fumigated for rats and bedbugs. And on hot summer nights they allowed the older girls and women to sleep out in the courtyard because of overcrowding, never mind the mosquitoes and other fleas. Charlie had never once gone to sleep outside because that was where a lot of the abuse had happened. Ragland had warned her to never expose herself in that way. But no one spoke of the horrible abuses inflicted on the girls and women for fear of terrible repercussions.

But she was finally free and would never again put her life at the mercy of anyone else. She spotted an empty bench, for she had no desire to speak to anyone and made her way to it. There was an old newspaper lying on it, clearly having wrapped chips and fish from the smell. The one thing Charlie loved to do was read even though her options had been very limited at the workhouse.

"A good education will take you far," Ragland had told her time and time again as he brought her old books and newspapers. She had found a loose tile on the dormitory floor and that had been her hiding spot for a long time. Good thing was that no one ever bothered to repair that damaged floor and she now had two books in her possession that she'd read over and over again. Charlie had no idea where Ragland had found the copies of Oliver Twist and Nicholas Nickleby, all written by the famous writer Charles Dickens. Though many of the pages were missing, she had grasped the gist of the stories and identified herself with the two boys who had been ill used by their relatives. "That's why I want you to promise me that you'll never stop learning," Ragland had told her when she shared her feelings about Oliver and Nicholas with him. "So you can defeat all those who ill-treated you." Charlie had made the promise to her friend and now she was grateful to him because though she hadn't received any formal education, she was better than most of her peers. She could read and write very well, and she intended to continue learning as a befitting tribute to the young man who had been her best and probably only good friend.

Her eyes returned to the newspaper cutting which was an advertisement by some clothing factory in Manchester. She nearly tossed it away when she noticed that they mentioned that they needed seamstresses. That was her forte and she wondered if she would be offered a position should she show up. There was no date on the newspaper, so she had no idea when the advertisement had been placed. But it got her thinking. She had money and felt her pocket for the envelope she'd slipped in it. It was still there, and she sighed in relief. Some of the women she'd been in the workhouse with had spoken of pickpockets lurking in every corner of London.

"There are some who are so skilled that they can strip you of all your clothing and you'll be none the wiser," one of the friendlier matrons had told them, clearly painting the sordid picture to

deter them from running away from the workhouse. Of course, Charlie and the others had listened with their mouths agog, and to her the streets of London were full of evils just waiting to pounce.

She took the envelope out of her pocket and counted the money. There was one pound and several shillings. This was what the last eight years of her life had been worth, and she shook her head. This was what Ragland and many others had died for. Someone would one day pay for all the terrible things that had happened in the workhouse. And even though she was enraged at the suffering, Charlie knew she was one of the very few lucky ones.

Many girls had been ravished by the male supervisors and made unwed mothers. Some girls had died during childbirth because of the terrible conditions in the workhouse, while others had ended their own lives. Unable to cope with the humiliation of having been forced to surrender their virtues, some girls ended their lives rather than live with the pain of continued abuse or unwanted pregnancies. But no one had ever been punished for those crimes.

"Just you wait," Charlie whispered. "Someday someone will avenge your sufferings and deaths," she spoke to those long gone, not that they would hear her, but it made her feel somewhat better.

Ragland had protected her, and it even surprised her that she'd walked out of the workhouse with her virtue still intact. Though it had been no mean feat. She would never forget the boy who had sacrificed his life just to keep her alive and safe.

"Oh Ragland."

Two years after his mother's death and the discovery that he was a boy, Ragland had managed to escape from the workhouse and ended up as a street urchin. But he was caught picking someone's pockets and brought back to the workhouse. He was fourteen at the time and never stopped thinking about his freedom. It was his great affection for Charlie that had stopped him from attempting another escape but sadly, just four years later, he was dead.

However, by that time he'd already learned how to work the system, the places to hide so he could be safe and how to obtain food in the midst of hunger and starvation. "Go well my friend," she murmured as she made the decision to travel to Manchester. She was done with Leeds forever.

POINT OF NO RETURN

M anchester – *Eight Months Later*

This was the one time of the year that she dreaded with her whole heart. In a bid to

escape the terrible memories the weeks approaching Christmas brought, Charlie tried everything. From taking on extra work so she'd be too exhausted to think to locking herself up and forcing sleep on herself, she did all she could to keep all the bad thoughts out of her mind.

Sadly, she had found out that no matter how hard she tried to erase the memories, they just wouldn't fade away. And worse, the pain remained the same. Like everyone else, she tried to live in the present, but the past would never let her be. It was a part of her life that followed her everywhere like an unwavering shadow. The pain was so deep that she felt physically ill just thinking about it. She would never escape from the dark memories and the terrible dreams that haunted her during this season.

Someone, she couldn't quite recall who, had once said that with time pain gets less and scars fade. Charlie laughed, a brittle sound that startled the woman standing next to her. But she was oblivious to anything other than her pain. No, pain never went away, and in her case, it only grew worse with the passing years.

And with the pain came the realisation that the scars she carried in her heart and body would never fade away. And speaking of scars,

Charlie raised both hands and stared at her deformed fingers. Burning anger settled deep within her heart and her lips tightened. They would pay, and that was a promise! Every last one of them would pay for the pain, anguish and humiliation they had subjected her to. With each passing day Charlie thought about ways of inflicting deep pain on those who had hurt her and the ideas took on very frightening forms with each new day.

"It's just a matter of time," she muttered to herself.

"Charlotte did you say something?" Martha Wilkins asked. Though they were nearly the same age Charlie never considered Martha to be a friend even though they were colleagues and had the same job. The two women were tallying clerks in charge of keeping records of all the manufactured goods in their section. Charlie's fast rise to this position was because of her ability to read and write and she never stopped giving thanks for Ragland's insistence that she learn both. This was considered a high-end job, and the pay was much better than what those who worked on the factory floors got. Also, it wasn't as back-breaking, and since she and Martha were the only women who were literate, they shared a small office. Martha tried to make friends with her, but Charlotte Weston had no friends, nor did she need anyone in her life. So she turned ice cold eyes to Martha, who'd shivered slightly.

"What did you ask me?"

"I asked if you had said something," Martha's hands twitched nervously as she picked up the folder on the table in front of her.

"No I didn't say anything," Charlie's voice was even colder.

Martha bowed her head and went on counting the garments in the crate at her feet. Like everyone else in the finishing department of Baden Textile Industries, Martha was terrified of Charlie. Her eyes were so cold, and no one had ever seen her smile, even though she'd been working at the factory for close to eight months now. Everyone shied away from working too closely with her and it was only the gentle Martha who had agreed to work with Charlie, albeit reluctantly. But even then, Charlie rarely spoke to her colleague unless it was absolutely necessary.

Paul Vermont observed the two female tallying clerks in the packing section and frowned slightly. He'd just brought in two bundles of finished garments and found them standing and facing each other as if they were having an argument. The shorter one looked really nervous while the tall one pierced her with a glare.

And as if the two became aware of his scrutiny both of them turned and fixed their eyes on him. The shorter woman turned away quickly, while the taller one continued staring at him as if she was daring him to speak to her.

"Who is that lady," he asked his colleague without once taking his eyes off the tall woman.

"That is the ice maiden as we all call her around here," the man snickered then shivered. "Frankly speaking, she should be called the woman with the coldest eyes on earth."

"Come on Joseph you're exaggerating, I don't see anything cold about her eyes though they are fascinating." Paul turned away for a split second to look at his colleague and when he looked back the woman was gone. His eyes searched around the large warehouse for her, but he couldn't find her. He was really fascinated by the woman's deep blue eyes.

"I'm telling you the truth," Joseph held up one hand. "Some people say her stare can turn a man into stone like the mythical Medusa."

Paul chuckled softly as he lifted a bale of finished garments onto his shoulders. "Come on and stop it with all that Greek mythology nonsense. We better go and bring in the other lot of finished garments before the supervisor comes looking for us. I'll look for the blue-eyed woman later."

"My friend," Joseph followed him out of the warehouse. "Listen to me, if you know what's good for you, you'll stay away from that one. No one dares to get close to her, not even the other ladies. She shows up to work very early, does her tallying as required, and all without speaking a single word to anyone. And when she's done she locks up her books and walks out of the factory alone. People say she returns to the sea from whence she has come."

Paul shook his head at his colleague's blabbering. The one thing he was quickly finding out was that a lot of gossip went on in the factory. If one wanted information about anything that was going on, all they had to do was to start a conversation with any of the loaders, the packer or even the seamstresses. Everyone always had something to say about any matter put before them. Paul's curiosity about the tall woman was piqued and he found himself wanting to find out more about her. This was quite strange for him because in all his twenty-six years of life no woman had ever captured his interest like this one. *Ice maiden indeed,* he thought to himself. He would prove to everyone that the girl had a heart just like everyone else.

STRANGE FEELINGS

Charlie felt like she'd just escaped from a threatening situation. Her heart was pounding so hard and her hands were shaking. Her palms were sweaty, and she couldn't believe that the single stare of a man could unnerve her so much. This had never happened to her before and she couldn't believe that she had just run away from a staring match if one could call it that. Usually, it was the other party who turned away first. But looking into those deep grey eyes had made her feel something really strange within her stomach, like thousands of butterflies were fluttering around inside there. When she felt calm enough, she returned to her usual place of work and resumed counting the garments in one crate. It was tedious and monotonous work, but she always told herself that she was better off than most of her age mates who worked on the factory floor.

"You look rattled," Martha came up suddenly behind her, startling her.

"Martha, I've told you several times to stop coming up so suddenly behind me. Do you want to get hurt?"

Martha gave her a nervous smile. "I'm sorry, I didn't mean to startle you. Are you all right? You took off running like someone was after you, and I got a bit concerned."

Charlie turned to look at the woman who was the only one who dared come close to her. The others either steered clear or made disparaging remarks whenever she went by. But one thing was clear; Charlie clearly intimidated everyone, including the supervisors. No one had ever won a staring match against her, until today. Who was that man and why had he been staring at them?

"Charlie, are you all right?" Martha repeated her question, and Charlie raised her eyes. She was surprised to see genuine concern in the other woman's eyes. No one had ever showed any concern for her wellbeing other than Ragland, and it made her quite uncomfortable. She wasn't used to being treated with kindness, so she didn't know how she was supposed to behave with Martha, who was the epitome of meekness and gentleness. So she chose to either ignore the woman altogether or be downright rude and unapproachable. But still Martha continued trying to get close to her. She didn't need this, not at all. No one made friends with another unless there was something to be gained. This woman clearly needed something from her, else why would she pretend to be nice?

In Charlie's experience, no one was ever nice to another unless they wanted something in return. It had surprised her that Martha seemed to have attached herself to her from the moment she had arrived at Baden Textile Factory nearly eight months ago. No amount of her being rude or snubbing Martha had sent the woman away like it had done for everyone else. Either Martha Wilkins was a glutton for punishment or else she had some ulterior motive for wanting to be close to Charlie.

"Martha, what is it you want from me?" Charlie's tone was chilly.

"I don't know what you mean," there was genuine puzzlement on Martha's face. "We work together and that means that we spend a lot of time together six days a week. Is it a bad thing if I think that we can be more than just workmates?"

"Not if that's all it is."

"What else could it be?"

"Look, if you're seeking someone to gossip with, or meet during the weekends and go shopping or all the other nonsense women like doing then you have the wrong person. I don't do the kinds of things other people do because frankly speaking they don't hold any appeal for me. If all you want to be is a good colleague and workmate then so be it, but I reserve my judgment insofar as the two of us being friends goes. You will need things from me that I'm not able to give you and then you'll get offended and that might then strain our working relationship," Charlie turned away to carry on with her work. This woman was seeking more than she was willing to give and she needed to know that Charlie just wasn't interested.

"Charlie," Martha drew closer and placed a hand on Charlie's arm and the next thing she knew, she was practically flying across the room and Charlie's stance immediately became combative, as if she were ready to defend herself from some kind of attack.

"I'm sorry," Martha cowered against the wall where she'd landed after the surprise attack on her person. She had never seen such a violent reaction from an innocent touch before.

"I warned you to never come up behind me," Charlie hissed.

"What's going on here?" Paul had just walked in with another crate when he heard the commotion and rushed in. From the way the short woman was cowering and the tall one had her arms raised like a pugilist, it was clear that an altercation had just happened. "Ladies, what is going on here?" He repeated his question.

Charlie blinked and Paul's face came into focus. She slowly lowered her hands but even as they fell to her sides Paul could see that her fists were still clenched though not all her fingers were bent.

"I'm sorry," Charlie looked at Martha who Paul was helping to get back on her feet. "But don't ever do that again or you could be seriously injured," and saying thus, Charlie turned and walked out of the warehouse. She was glad it was a rather slow day at the warehouse or else many people would have witnessed whatever had gone on, and that would have created a different kind of trouble. Fighting or arguing in public was an offence that could cause one to immediately lose their job or else be suspended from work without pay. Charlie couldn't afford to lose any of her wages. A lot was riding on her saving enough money so she could put all her plans into action. She didn't need to get into any trouble, but Martha had been asking for it by sneaking up behind her, even though she'd warned her several times never to do that.

Paul turned to the much-shaken woman. "What happened with your friend?"

Martha gave a small nervous laugh in response, "Friend? I wouldn't call Charlie my friend. That woman has no friends."

"Charlie?"

"Her name is Charlotte Weston, but everyone calls her Charlie, not that she ever responds."

"Why were you fighting? Do you know that if one of the other supervisors had walked in on this scene the two of you would have lost your jobs without question? Fighting is one of the incidents that will get you terminated without any further explanation."

"We weren't fighting," Martha protested mildly. She looked like she was about to burst into tears and Paul felt sorry for her.

"What's your name?"

"Martha Wilkins, and I promise you that we weren't fighting."

"So then what happened in here? I walked in on a very frightening scene, and it concerns me a lot. The two of you seemed to be getting along well but this is cause for alarm."

"I saw that Charlie seemed agitated and simply asked her what the matter was. Then I touched her arm but didn't intend any harm to her. The next thing I knew, she had flung me over her shoulder, and I was flying across the room."

"And you're sure that you didn't provoke her at all?"

Martha shook her head, "I'm telling you the truth, I didn't provoke her at all."

Paul nodded. "Get back to work then and don't tell anyone about what happened here, not even your friends. If it comes out that there was an altercation between the two of you, your jobs could be in jeopardy."

"Please no," Martha's voice was filled with fear. "I really need this job. My husband was laid off from the shoe factory where he worked because of his ill health and hasn't been able to find anything since. So my salary is all we have, I can't lose this position."

"Don't worry," Paul's voice was soothing. "I won't tell anyone what happened here. But you need to be very careful that something like this doesn't happen again."

"Believe me," Martha shuddered visibly. "I'm never coming anywhere near Charlie again. One fright was enough, thank you."

"Would you like to be transferred to another department?"

Martha looked at Paul with surprise. "Aren't you just one of the packers or loaders? How then do you sound as if you have influence with the supervisors in here?"

Paul chuckled, "One of them is my friend and that's how I even got this job that I'm doing," he lowered his eyes in an effort to look very humble. "He's a good person and if I tell him that you're having trouble with your colleague then he'll find you somewhere else to work."

Martha smiled, "Please don't go to all that much trouble on my behalf. Besides, I don't want it said by the supervisors that I'm a troublemaker. If I change departments then it will look as if I'm the one who is on the wrong."

"Are you sure about that?"

"Yes, I'll be all right. I just have to be careful not to provoke Charlie in any way and I'll be sure to stay out of her way from now going forward."

When Charlie walked out of the warehouse and left Martha with the man who was causing her to have butterflies in her stomach, she prayed that she wouldn't run into any of the supervisors who were sure to ask her why she wasn't at her usual post. So she hid herself and sneaked to the back of the warehouse where she leaned tiredly against the wall. She was trembling at what had nearly happened. She'd nearly hurt an innocent woman who was just concerned about her. Martha's only crime had been touching her to offer comfort.

Charlie avoided any contact with anyone, and she shuddered, raising her hands which were still shaking.

"Be careful of your temper," she heard one of the workhouse matrons' voices in her head. *"You have so much rage within you that you can decapitate a person with your mere hands."*

At the time the supervisor was sounding that warning, Charlie had hit a male supervisor who was bigger than her. He'd been saying terrible things about Ragland who'd only recently been buried. He'd actually called Ragland her husband and that had enraged Charlie. By the time nearly four people had pulled her off the young man, his nose was broken and both his eyes were swollen and shutting from the blows she'd inflicted on him. She had no idea where all that strength had come from and she had reacted to the bully's words and actions.

Before that he'd followed her when she was going to the outhouse and tried to touch her inappropriately, teasing her that her 'husband' was dead and buried and could no longer defend her. She'd flown into a rage and it was his screams that had brought the other children running. When they were unable to get her off of him, they had also screamed and the four supervisors both male and female had broken up the one-sided fight.

But from that day, no one had tried to get close to her, and for the remaining two years in the workhouse she had been put in an isolated room away from the other children. She later realised that the matron who had taken her away from the others had in her own way been looking out for her. Not that the punishments had ended, but at least she was safe from all the inappropriate touching by the male supervisors.

Charlie took a deep breath to calm herself down and when she was sure that she was in control of her senses and emotions once again, she returned to the tallying office.

"I'm sorry Martha," she said, surprised to find the other woman still working. She'd expected her to run screaming out of the warehouse demanding to be placed elsewhere.

"You scared me so much, Charlie."

"It will never happen again but please stay as far away from me as you possibly can. I don't ever want to hurt you."

Martha gave her a gentle smile as if understanding her and Charlie felt guilty that she hadn't been nicer to her. "I know that you never intended to harm me, and I promise that I won't ever startle you again, at least not intentionally. Please be patient with me."

"Thank you."

MEDUSA TAMED

Charlie sensed his presence even before she saw him and felt her whole body tense up.

"Charlotte," the deep voice hailed her and she had no idea whether it was a greeting or she was being summoned so she didn't immediately respond. "Miss Charlotte Weston, my name is Paul…."

Charlie slowly turned around and looked into the piercing grey eyes that gave her sleepless nights from the first time she'd looked into them. It was as if he were seeing right into her very soul, and that made her very uncomfortable.

"If I knew your name then I would respond by calling it out like you've done with mine," her usual reaction to situations that scared her was to lash out. She gave him the coldest look she could muster and to her surprise, instead of getting angry at the brush off like other men did, he simply threw his head back and laughed. She felt her face turning red and wished Martha would quickly return from wherever it was that she'd gone.

"You weren't paying attention because I was just trying to tell you my name." He entered further into their small office and she immediately felt like he was crowding her. "My name is Paul Vermont if you care to know."

"A man of your position shouldn't be inside this office, as it's out of bounds to loaders and packers," she barked out. "In any case, there's plenty of work to be done out there without you coming in here for a gossip session. Get back to work at once or else the supervisor will hear of your insolence."

"Yes Ma'am," Paul said subserviently, but the look in his eyes made her feel that he was laughing at her.

"Run along now," she said scathingly, waving a hand like one would to shoo away an annoying puppy. Then she turned and picked up the papers she'd been working on but all the while aware of his continued presence. When she heard his footsteps moving away, she sagged with relief.

What was it about this man that shook her and made her feel so unsettled? She had looked into many other men's eyes and seen wickedness and the desire to possess, and not in a good way. Yet when she had looked into Paul Vermont's eyes, she hadn't felt intimidated or scared of him and what he could use his strength for, since he was a tall and well-built man. No, she'd felt reassured by his presence and something that felt like safety.

"What is happening to me?" Charlie murmured as she picked up the tallying papers. Martha walked into the office just then, and for the first time, Charlie gave her a tight smile.

"Why Charlie, I believe you just smiled at me," Martha teased but was careful to stay on the other side of the office. "It's never happened before and this day might well end better than it started."

"Martha you exaggerate," Charlie was trying her best to be a better colleague. Ever since the tense incident of a few days ago, a wall seemed to have come down between the two women. It wasn't that they were headed toward being friends or anything. But Charlie was less hostile toward Martha. On her part, Martha seemed to have lost quite a bit of the nervousness that she often displayed around Charlie. Though she was now very careful to announce her presence with a loud greeting before she got close.

Paul returned to work with a smile on his face. The Ice Maiden wasn't as frightening as he'd been told to expect. No, he'd seen something like deep pain in her eyes before she blinked. It was clear that something in her past or maybe even her present-day life had caused her a lot of pain. Maybe that was the reason she was very hostile to everyone around her. He knew from interacting with some ladies in church that an abused person tended to always be defensive and would easily react violently to any threats whether real or perceived.

Paul was determined that he would be the one who would break down all the barriers so the sweet and innocent girl lurking behind the hostile and unapproachable woman could break through and be free. Charlotte Weston was worth fighting for and he would win her back from whatever it was that held her captive.

Over the next few days, Charlie noticed that Paul seemed to turn up everywhere she was. He was always in her tallying office more frequently that anyone else, and Martha even began to comment on his presence.

"If I didn't know well enough, I'd think that loader man is seeking your attention."

"He's just wasting his time," Martha said in annoyance. His presence was quite unnerving and unsettling, and she was beginning to make mistakes in her tallying reports.

"He looks like a good person," Martha said.

Charlie merely shrugged, wondering where he would turn up next. When she stepped out for a breath of fresh air, there he was. During mealtimes he would be at the table next to hers, and his eyes seemed to always monitor her movements.

But there was a positive side to his unwanted attention. The men who had previously harassed and made life uncomfortable for her seemed to have eased off. If anything, they regarded her with some sort of deference. It made her relieved that she didn't have to always be on her guard around the warehouse anymore.

"I must be a fool," she murmured to herself more than once when she found her eyes searching for him. Something was happening inside her, and it terrified her. She'd never felt this way about any man before and it bothered her that Paul disturbed her peace. Not even Ragland had evoked such strong feelings within her, and he was the only man who had come very close to her. Since she had no friends—not even Martha could be considered that—she had no one to confide in, so she struggled with her feelings, suffering in silence.

Paul on his part began to sense that Charlie was thawing toward him and had noticed that whenever their eyes met, hers weren't as frosty as a sea covered in ice. But he also knew that it would be a long time before Charlie completely lowered her guard and allowed him to get close to her. Still, he found that more and more each day, he was developing very strong feelings toward her.

Finally, one day hc decided to make a direct approach to her. It was the last week of November and the weather was getting worse with each passing day. And darkness seemed to descend much earlier each day. The sun rarely came out and it rained heavily nearly every day. Newspapers were forecasting a lot of snow this year and warning everyone to be careful about dangerous drifts.

Since it was just a few weeks to the end of the year, the volume of work had increased. They were in a hurry to do as much as possible before the holidays really descended upon them. The factory would remain closed from the twenty-third of December up to the second day of the New Year.

Everyone seemed to be in a hurry to leave the factory on that particular day, and Paul waited for Charlie who was one of the last to step out of the large gates.

"Do you have far to walk?" He fell into step beside her and nearly smiled at the surprise on her face when she turned and saw him.

"What is it to you?" She asked rudely, wishing him away because his nearness was causing havoc to her heart. "And where do you think you're going?" She demanded when he refused to be shaken off.

"It's getting dark and I want to be sure that you get home safely."

"There are many other women who are walking home alone and would most definitely enjoy your company."

"Well, none of them are you," Paul said. "Don't imagine that your rudeness will chase me away. If anything, it only makes me want to find out what has caused such a sweet woman like you to be so cold and unsmiling. Your eyes and lips were made for smiling, Miss Charlotte Weston."

"Flattery will get you nowhere, Mr. Paul Vermont. And besides, I like walking home alone because my own company is preferable to bothersome companions. All you want to do is gossip but please be informed that I won't indulge you."

"No woman can remain as an island forever, Miss Weston. And you're too beautiful to be all alone. Is it perhaps a harsh father who makes you shun everyone? Does he forbid you from making friends?"

Paul was shocked when Charlie turned and lashed out hard. If he wasn't quick on his feet, the blow would have landed on his face.

"Don't ever mention that name to me again," and her voice was cold and her eyes shuttered. She turned and hurried away, so Paul found himself letting out his breath even as he followed her discreetly. Thankful for the cover of darkness, he was able to keep a few paces behind her, eyes alert in case anyone else wanted to get up to some mischief by following her.

Charlie got the feeling that someone was following her, but it didn't occur to her that it could be Paul. After striking out at him, she expected that he had fled. No man wanted to deal with a woman who was ready to hit him. She began to regret why she'd been so nasty to the man when all he'd wanted to do was to see her safely home. He wasn't to know that she never spoke about her family and especially her father. That man was dead to her, they all were. Thinking or speaking about them only evoked very painful memories that she would rather forget.

Her heart was pounding as she practically ran the few remaining yards to the small boarding house where she'd lived ever since she arrived in Manchester. It was run by an elderly woman, and she had a very strict policy of not allowing anyone to come home when it was too dark.

"Stop," a hand grabbed her as she was just a step or two away from the front door and she screamed, struggling to free herself. Her purse dropped and she tried to twist away so she could launch herself at her assailant.

"Leave me alone," she sobbed.

"Miss Weston, it's me," Paul had to repeat nearly three times before his words penetrated through her terror-filled mind and she slumped, the fight suddenly drained out of her. Then she got angry once more.

"What were you thinking frightening me like that," there was a lantern on the small porch, but its light was weak. The street was dark save for a single gas lamp whose light was also not very bright. "You really scared me."

"I'm really sorry about that," Paul released her once he was sure she wouldn't flee suddenly. "That's the reason I wanted to walk you home," he turned to watch the street, eyes narrowed as two drunkards staggered by shouting obscenities to anyone they caught sight of. "I don't like this place you live in."

"I've been all right so far," Charlie was still angry at him. "And I don't need you or anyone else following me around and scaring me half to death."

"You've been all right so far because you've been leaving work while there's still light outside. I could have been someone else out to harm you."

And they would have been sorry, Charlie thought but didn't voice the words out loud. She also acknowledged that his words were true. But she wasn't sure what his motives were for insisting on seeing her home. Well, if he expected her to invite him into the house, then he was in for a big disappointment. He would be grossly mistaken to think she could trust him.

"I don't invite strangers into the house. Besides that, my landlady doesn't allow us ladies who live with her to bring men back into the house. She's that strict."

"That's all right, and it's even late now to invite anyone for a visit. All I wanted was to make sure that you got home safely. I'll be taking my leave now so please go in." He saw the curtain in the front window move. "Someone is watching out for you."

Charlie nodded curtly, then walked to the door, aware of Paul's unnerving gaze even in the darkness. Once she felt the doorknob turning she looked back. "Thank you, Mr. Vermont."

"I'll see you tomorrow and have a good night."

"Who was that man, Charlotte," Mrs. Kincaid moved away from the window as soon as Charlie entered the house. "I've never seen him before, and you know that I don't like you bringing strangers to the house."

"I'm sorry about that, Mrs. Kincaid. Paul Vermont is one of the workers at the factory and he escorted me home because it was dark."

"I thought you were fighting because I heard you cry out."

"No, I stepped on something and he was concerned," she didn't want the woman to know what had happened. "I'm sorry that we disturbed you."

"Not really, I was just worried because your friends are all in their rooms and you hadn't come in yet. It gets dark earlier these days, and the rainy and snow season are upon us. You shouldn't be staying out until dark. This isn't a safe street and I wouldn't want anything bad to happen to you."

"I promise that I'll be very careful."

"Good. Now go and wash up like your friends. Supper is about to be served, and as you know, we don't like to wait for anyone."

"Thank you, Ma'am."

That night as Charlie lay in bed in her small room, she smiled in the darkness. Mrs. Kincaid insisted on all candles being blown out by eight o'clock. The house was two storied, and the woman had her own large bedroom downstairs. The kitchen, parlour and living room were also downstairs. Upstairs were six bedrooms for her six boarders. Charlie's room contained a narrow bed, a small table and chair and a chest of drawers for her clothes. There was no closet, and she was expected to fold everything neatly and put it out of sight.

Charlie was happy because she had a room to herself and a good one at that. She remembered how life had been at the workhouse and shuddered. Forced to share a bed with three other girls before she'd been isolated for fighting, she'd never thought she would ever get her own bed. This was luxury in comparison to the attic back at her father's house and the dormitory at the workhouse.

"One day, I'll build a big house and have a very large bedroom," she murmured turning on her side. Then her thoughts took her back to Paul and she felt her face getting hot. Why was she thinking about that good-for-nothing man who was trouble itself? She would have to make sure that he never came close to the house again because she didn't want Mrs. Kincaid to get upset. Charlie acknowledged that she was luckier than most of the other women who worked at the factory. Other boarding houses were overcrowded, and she'd once heard a woman say that she had to share a tiny room with three other women, and it was really stuffy. Also, overcrowding meant lack of security, and a number of women at the factory had complained that they kept losing their properties.

Here in Mrs. Kincaid's house everyone had a key to their room. No one could enter another person's room without her permission. Yes, she was really lucky to have found this place, and she wouldn't do anything to jeopardise her stay here.

THAWING HEART

Paul looked at Charlie and felt a tug at his heart. She was smiling at the flower he'd given her. Given that it was winter, finding flowers had been difficult as they were all buried beneath the snow. But he'd found one and it gave him much joy to see Charlie's joy over the small gesture. They were seated in a small teahouse in town. He would have preferred to sit outside but it was very cold, and he could see that the snow had started falling. Getting Charlie to agree to come with him had taken him days of begging if he could call it that. She always had one excuse or the other but finally she'd given in on this Saturday morning.

"Why are you looking at me like that?" She raised her face and he was delighted to see her blushing. "Stop doing that."

"I've never seen you smiling genuinely, Charlie," he said. "And we've been working together for a few weeks now. You should do that more often."

The smile faded and sadness crept into her eyes. "People only smile when they have good reasons to do so."

"Charlie," Paul's voice softened, "There are many reasons for you to be smiling."

"Really?" Her voice was raspy and she cleared her throat. "Name one or two of those reasons."

"For one, the fact that we're alive and healthy should make you smile more. Think of those hundreds of people who are ill because of the terrible weather and some can't even leave their beds. Others can barely breathe, while many are lying dead in morgues all over the county. We have a lot to be thankful for, Charlie."

"Those are just ordinary, everyday situations," she scoffed.

"No, my dear," Paul said. "Ask anyone who is an invalid, ill or lame and has mutilated limbs what they most wish for. They will all tell you that good health and the chance to move around unimpeded is what they all long for. We can never take that for granted," Charlie was quietly listening to him. He watched as she raised the small flower to her face to breathe in its scent. "Also, just think about this, Christmas Season is upon us and it's a very special time for everyone because of what the Lord did for us. If there's nothing else we can be thankful for at this time of the year, let's remember to smile about Christmas and all the promises fulfilled in that holiday."

Charlie shuddered and turned away. Paul observed her for a while, noticing that her hands were clenched together, though she was careful not to bruise the flower.

"What happened to make you react so negatively to my mentioning Christmas?"

"It's the worst time of the year and I just wish it would come and go without me being aware of it."

"I don't understand. With all the cheer in the air, the smell of baking gingerbread and cookies, garlands adorning doorways and children singing carols. How can you not enjoy this season?" His eyes roamed around the small teahouse. "Even this place is already setting the mood for Christmas," he pointed at a small tree in one of the corners even though there were no decorations on it yet.

"Because," she gasped, standing up abruptly. Her chest was heaving, and she felt like screaming. Why was this man reminding her of the pain she was trying so hard to bury? "I have to leave now." She ignored the waitress who was bringing their tea.

"Charlie," Paul was always careful not to touch her because each time his hand drew closer, she flinched and pulled away. Someone had really done a lot of damage to this woman, but he refused to let her continue living in her protective shell. "Please calm down because I didn't mean to get you so worked up. Forgive me. Sit and have a cup of hot tea and then I promise that I'll walk you home."

"I have to get back home now," she said and walked away. Paul shook his head sadly. He'd thought that he was finally breaking through the barriers and getting to Charlie's heart. It seemed like he still had a long way to go.

"Lord, please show me what to do to help my friend. She is hurting so much, and I wish she could find peace, especially as we approach this special season when we celebrate the birth of Your beloved and loving Son, Jesus Christ. Charlie needs you so much, Lord. Let this be the year that she gets relief from all the pain she's carried within her and walks into freedom."

He nodded at the bewildered waitress. "It wasn't your fault, she had to leave in a hurry but I'll pay for everything," and he did so, also leaving a generous tip for the anxious girl.

The next Monday evening, Charlie was surprised to find Paul waiting to walk her home, and it showed on her face.

"Why do you look so surprised to see me?" He asked.

"I thought you wouldn't want to speak to me ever again after I walked away from you at the teahouse on Saturday. I'm sorry, but you upset me with all that talk about Christmas."

"Charlie, I would never abandon you, not unless I'm too ill to walk with you and see you safely to your residence."

"Oh!" She was lost for words.

"Let's go."

It took Charlie a few days to open up to Paul, and she did it on Sunday afternoon just five days before Christmas Day. According to management at the factory, they would be closing down in two days so people could travel and be with their families. But she had nowhere to go so she would be spending her Christmas Day with Mrs. Kincaid, her landlady. The other five girls who lived in the same boarding house had plans of travelling and were all so excited about seeing their families again. Charlie refused to envy those who had loving families waiting for them. Martha had even tried to invite her to her house, but she'd shut that down firmly.

Paul had finally convinced her to accompany him to church that Sunday morning, even coming to meet her at Mrs. Kincaid's house. Coming to church was just to get Paul off her back because he kept asking her to join him and she'd put him off enough times.

The church was much larger than the one back home in Wetherby but just as imposing. She mumbled greetings to other congregants who insisted on stopping to greet them. She could see that Paul was on very good terms with so many of them.

"The service usually lasts for about one and a half hours. I hope you won't get bored," he said when they were are the church door. "I sometimes sing in the choir and may be asked to join them. I don't want you to feel neglected."

"You do what you have to do," she said as she followed him inside and immediately regretted that she had allowed him to convince her to come. She noticed that men and women didn't sit on the same side. He walked her to one of the middle pews and after she had sat down, he walked across and took his own seat.

Charlie noticed people giving her curious looks, but she chose to ignore them, her eyes roaming all over the sanctuary. There were no paintings on the walls, but large windows with stained glass took up most of the space making the inside very bright. If she hadn't been feeling uncomfortable, she might have appreciated the beauty of the place, which seemed to have so much life. The small church back in Wetherby had been dark and draughty, and she had hated it. And for the eight years that she'd been in the workhouse, all the services had been held in the dining hall because there was no chapel close by.

"I can do this," she told herself as she tried to settle down. Two women came in and moved to sit next to her. She bowed her head as if in deep prayer so they wouldn't speak to her.

But even before the service began, she felt too uncomfortable and walked out. There were concrete benches scattered along the open walkway and in the church gardens. She spotted one under an awning close to a small building a short distance from the main church and it was to that one that she headed, sitting down heavily. The scowl on her face forbade anyone from speaking to her, and they hurried toward the church leaving her to her own devices.

It was cold but so was her heart, and she felt numb inside. She didn't want anyone to tell her all that nonsense about a God who loved people. Where had he been all her life when she'd endured so much pain and torment at the hands of her family? It was the large cross at the front of the church that had triggered all her anger. Where had the loving God been in the eight years that she'd spent at that terrible workhouse, fighting with all she had to live to see another day and preserve her dignity as a woman?

"You can't be there," she hissed through clenched teeth. "Those who believe in God are only deluding themselves and refusing to face the reality that everyone can only depend on him- or herself," she muttered.

A sudden flash of lightning and loud clap of thunder startled her and she nearly fell off the bench on which she was seated. Even as a child she'd hated storms and feared being struck by lightning. She remembered the day long ago when her stepmother had locked her out of the house and made her stand in the heavy rain just because she'd wet her bed out of fear. She'd only been five at the time and unlike her siblings who had chamber pots in their rooms, she was expected to make her way out of the house alone in the darkness to the outhouse. On that day she'd been beaten up and her stepmother had made one of the servants drag all her soiled beddings out to the backyard even though it had been raining.

"You like wetness, let's see how you like standing in the rain," she had shouted. Charlie had begged her not to leave her out in the open with the flashing lightning and booming thunder, but her pleas and cries had gone unheeded.

She covered her ears and buried her face on her lap so she wouldn't hear the thunder in her ears. And that was how Paul found her nearly an hour and a half later when the service was over. He approached her cautiously knowing that she might jump up and lash out if he startled her.

"Charlotte," he called out softly and was relieved when she looked up, her face white and tense. "What's wrong?"

"I hate thunder and lightning," she said. "Can you take me home now?" She was shivering because of the cold. The wind had caused the rain to blow over her and her clothes were wet. She started to rise but he shook his head. "Don't you want to walk me home? I'll go alone."

"I'm going to sit down beside you and pray that you won't feel intimidated enough to hit me," he stood there waiting for her to give her permission. She finally nodded and sat back down, folding her arms across her chest to ward off the cold but she was quite chilled.

"It's very cold," her teeth chattered. "I think I should just go home," she said but made no move to rise up to her feet again.

"Here," Paul handed her his thick coat and when she hesitated, he placed it on her knees. It was warm and Charlie nearly groaned out loud with happiness. It was large as he was, and she pulled it up to her chin.

"I hope I don't get it wet," she said. "Won't you feel cold?" She asked him, while hoping he wouldn't change his mind and ask for his coat back, at least not so soon.

"I have this inner coat and scarf so no, I'll be all right for now, though we can't stay out here for too long." They sat in silence for a while. "Why did you walk out of the church before the service had even begun? Did someone offend you or look at you judgmentally?"

Charlie was silent for so long that he thought she'd fallen asleep with her eyes wide open. But she turned her head slightly and then went on gazing at the steadily falling rain.

"How will people get home in this rain?" She asked. "I saw some little children; how will their parents get them home?"

"Many of them have umbrellas, and others their carriages. Those without one or the other will have to wait out the rain inside the church. And then there are those who don't mind getting wet so they will walk through the rain. Why do you ask?"

Charlie shrugged, "Nothing really, I was just curious to know how people intend to get home today."

"You haven't answered my question, Charlie. Why did you agree to come to church with me but walked out before the preacher came in?"

"Because I don't believe in all that nonsense being shouted from the pulpit by some man who wants everyone to believe that he is a saint. It's all lies, and no one should be forced to listen to all that deceit," she said in a harsh whisper as she saw some people walking toward them. She waited until they had passed by and went round the small building. Once they were out of sight, she resumed her tirade. "There is no such thing as a loving God. If there's a deity up there, then He's not a loving Being at all. If you all claim that God is love, then why are there such terrible people in the world who live only to hurt others?" She turned angry eyes on Paul who looked at her with so much tenderness that it unnerved her. "Stop looking at me like I've lost my mind."

"Charlie, please calm down."

"No, I won't calm down," she felt like there was something within that wanted to burst out. She had no idea that she was so angry or there was so much pent up emotion in her heart. "Why do you believe in all those myths?"

"What myths?"

"Christmas, Passover and all the other nonsense about Christianity; those time-wasting holidays you people always gush about. A loving God wouldn't let people suffer, and especially not innocent children," she didn't realise that she was crying until Paul reached out a hand and wiped away the tears. "You asked why I didn't sit and wait for the service, well I'll tell you." She moved away from him and then dashed away more tears with the back of her hand. "It's the hypocrisy of it all. All those people who show up to their churches every Sunday and on other Christian holidays are nothing but sanctimonious hypocrites."

"Why do you say that?" Paul was shocked at the vehemence in her voice, but it didn't show on his face. His voice remained gentle.

"Because I've lived that kind of life of going to church every Sunday and on other holidays, and I know that nothing those people say is true. A man and his wife take his children to church, sing hymns, recite prayers and then return home to abuse the servants and any unwanted children who live with them, forgetting all about the love they professed to have for everyone," she said mockingly.

"Charity begins at home is a fallacy if you ask me. I am very sure that not one of those people who attend church have any love in their hearts for anyone but themselves. Love the poor, take care of the weak, the vicars like to shout at the top of their heads but who ever does that in truth?"

"Is that what happened to you Charlie?"

"Yes," she hissed. "For ten years all I knew in my father's house was pain. Why didn't they just kill me and be done with me if they didn't want me? Why keep me alive day after day just to torture, humiliate and hurt me?"

Paul hadn't expected her to answer in the affirmative and he was shocked at the anguish he saw on her face. He longed to wipe her tears away, but she had moved, and he didn't want her to feel intimidated. "No one could kill you before your time, Charlie, because you're a child of destiny. The only One who can decide your future is the Lord, and unless the Lord decides that it's time for you to leave this earth, you're here to stay. Your life is in

His hands and no one has any control over that except the Lord Himself because He has a special purpose for your life."

"What purpose? What life?" Her voice rose, but she didn't care. Paul was glad that the rain had stopped and people had left. The churchyard was empty, and it seemed as if it was only the two of them left on the compound. "What purpose, I ask you?" Charlie demanded. "To be unwanted by one's own father? I never understood why my mother hated me so much all my life until I discovered who I really was and what my place in that family was," she was breathing hard. "My father's forced infidelity with one of the chambermaids led to my birth, and my poor mother only lived three days after I was born before she succumbed to despair and a broken body. Tortured by her mistress she lost all her will to live, so I came into this world as an unwanted child. My stepmother at first couldn't have children and my father forced himself on my mother just to have a child. But as soon as the poor chambermaid conceived, so did my stepmother and that was the beginning of hell for my mother. That's the world I came into and grew up in. So tell me again, what purpose has my life served until now?"

Paul felt her deep anguish and pain but said nothing. He knew that the only way that the woman he loved would begin to find healing was by facing her past, dealing with it and them putting it behind her.

"Beaten everyday by my father or stepmother, humiliated by my half siblings, tossed aside and discarded to a workhouse because I was unwanted," Charlie shook her head. "I was only ten years old when my father took me to Leeds and dumped me in a workhouse. He gave instructions that I was to never be let free until I turned eighteen," she wiped her face. "I think he believed that I wouldn't live that long and he would be well rid of me once and for all. Fighting for my life, my virtue and my dignity became the order of the day at the workhouse. Then worse, I lost my best friend and the only person who ever really cared about me because he died after falling from the roof of the workhouse. He died because he was protecting me from a man who would have destroyed my body and my dignity."

"I'm so sorry to hear that," Paul murmured. "Please don't be so angry."

"Sorry?" She laughed, a harsh sound that ripped at his heart. "Tell me Paul, what loving God would let a child go through all that? I never asked to be conceived and brought into this world. My mother never asked her master to force himself on her and put her in the family way and then turn against her once his wife had also conceived. And why did God choose to kill my mother when I needed her so much? Why didn't He just let me die at birth or even before I was properly formed in her womb?"

"Charlie..."

"Look at my fingers," she spread her hands out and folded her fingers. Two of them on each hand remained sticking out. They were crooked and completely disfigured, both bent at odd angles. "My fingers are deformed, and do you know why? Because I dared to love music which came naturally to me and I loved playing the piano so much. This was done to me by my stepmother when she realised that her children would never attain to my standards. I was only ten when she broke these two fingers, and no one got me any treatment. Instead, while I was delirious from the pain of broken bones, my father took me away from his house and dumped me at the workhouse. Tell me Paul, if you were the one, would you be sitting there and passing judgment on me because I'm angry at what happened to me?"

"Charlie, I can never judge you because I don't know what you have been through. And please forgive me if it seemed as if I were. What I want is to take your pain away, hold you in my arms and make a promise that no one will ever hurt you again. Will you please let me be the one that you lean on?"

At his gentle words, Charlie broke down completely and Paul couldn't hold himself any longer. He swiftly moved to her side and took her in his arms. She resisted at first, but the pain was too much for her to bear, and she finally collapsed on his chest.

"You'll be all right," he kept repeating as he gently stroked her hair. He felt deep anger at the way this poor young woman had been tortured by those who should have protected her. "All will be well."

WHERE IT ALL BEGAN

The moment Charlie stepped onto the soil of her father's estate she felt like darkness was about to overcome her. All the terrible memories of her life in this place rose up, and she moaned.

"I can't do this," she sobbed silently and turned to leave, wishing she hadn't quickly dismissed the carriage that had conveyed her here from the railway station. She had vowed to never set foot on this estate ever again but yet here she was. And it was all because her stupid heart had fallen in love with Paul and more than anything, she wanted to please him.

Paul! The man who'd made her break her vow and, in a way, compelled her to travel all the way back to Wetherby, West Yorkshire. And to the house of horrors, as she'd come to think of this place where she had grown up. From the outside nothing had changed except that the lawns were covered now in snow. Lawns which in springtime and summer had flowers she'd often tended when she lived at home. Rose bushes that had pricked her delicate hands, embedding thorns in her soft flesh and, with no one to remove them, sometimes they had festered and formed pus, causing her a lot of pain. Nothing had changed, but most of all, she dreaded meeting the inhabitants of the house. But for Paul, she wouldn't be here.

"I love you so much Charlie," he'd told her just two days ago after she'd broken down and given him her life's story. He'd held her in a comforting embrace as she poured her pain and anguish out in a torrent of tears. "And more than anything I want to marry you and spend the rest of my life with you. I have a ring that I bought from the moment I first saw you because there's something so special

about you and I know that God made you for me. But you carry so much pain and bitterness in your heart."

"And do you blame me?" She'd pulled away angrily from his arms. "With all that I've been through from the moment I was conceived, do you blame the anger that is within me?"

"No, not at all, my Love. But you need to be healed from all that pain and made whole again. Your heart was shattered, and your body was bruised and broken, and I can never imagine what you had to go through because my own childhood was regular and ordinary. I feel for you, Charlie, and more than anything, I want you to be made whole again. But that can only happen after you have faced the past, dealt with it and then put it behind you. That's only when you'll be able to move forward."

"You can keep your ring and your love because I never asked for it. And stay away from me," she got up and walked away from him, feeling enraged that he dared to judge her. How could he judge her when he'd never walked even a single step in her shoes?

But Paul had refused to give up on her like she'd expected, and the very next day, which was when the factory was being shut down for the holidays, he'd been waiting for her outside the gate as usual.

"Why do you keep bothering me?" She demanded. "Just leave me alone if all you want to do is preach to me about my past."

"Charlie, the last thing I will ever do is to abandon you. You may shout, insult or even hit me, but I'm not giving up on you," his eyes were so intense that she'd felt exposed. It was like he was stripping her heart bare, peeling away layer after layer of all the dark feelings that were inside and bringing them to light. But she saw genuine love and compassion, not like the pity she'd seen in the servants' eyes back in her father's house. They had pitied her but never once stepped forward to defend her against her parents or half siblings. Paul was different and something broke within her.

"Why won't you just give up on me? I'm a broken person and nothing can ever put me back together again."

"But that's not true, and I completely refuse to believe that," he cried out passionately. "There is hope for you, my Love" he said. "Even the Book of Job says that there is hope for a tree, if it be cut down, that it will sprout again, Charlie. And you are more than a tree, you are beloved of the Lord; a child of God."

"I don't know if that can be my life," she said brokenly, wishing more than anything that the pain within her would cease and she could be like other normal people. "How can that happen for me?"

"By forgiving...."

"What? You must be out of your mind to tell me something like that. I will never forgive all those who hurt me and destroyed my life, never!" She said vehemently.

"Charlie, as I told you yesterday, I carry a ring in my pocket, and it should be sitting on your finger."

"Which finger?" She said mockingly, holding up her deformed left-hand ring finger. "Can you imagine putting a pretty ring on this finger? It will look like putting a gold ring on the snout of a pig."

"Stop that at once, Charlie," his voice was harsh, and she flinched slightly. He hated seeing her look fearful, but he had to reach into her soul and remove all the darkness there even if it meant being somewhat harsh. "I won't have you degrading yourself like that. Let other misguided people do it because they are just unhappy individuals who derive satisfaction from putting other people down. But I won't let you do that to yourself," he took her hand and looked down at her finger. "This finger may be deformed but I love it like I love everything else about you. If the ring won't fit on this finger then we'll put it on another. But one way or another, you'll wear my engagement ring and eventually my wedding ring as well."

Charlie felt her breath catch in her throat as she raised her eyes to his and saw truth in them. "Paul, I'm not the woman you deserve...."

"Oh no, my treasured one, not that again. I love you so much and want you to be happy. But if there cannot be forgiveness in your heart then bitterness will fester and destroy you in the end. Holding onto your pain and not forgiving those who trespassed against you is putting yourself in prison. While you remain in that prison, they are living their lives to the fullest and you are missing out on so many blessings. My heart yearns for you and I really want to put this ring on your finger and declare to the whole world that we belong with each other. But that will only happen after you have made peace with your family back in Wetherby."

"Keep your ring and see if I care," she tried to walk away but he held onto her hand. She fought with the idea of forgiving her father, stepmother, half siblings, the wardens and supervisors at the workhouse. And she was also so angry at her mother for dying and leaving her to face this cruel world alone.

But Paul held on and kept murmuring soothing words, and she finally acknowledged that she, too, *was in love with him and wanted to be his wife. He was offering her the chance to have a family and be with someone who loved her so deeply. He'd told her about his own loving parents and three younger siblings, and she wanted to be a part of such a family. So she had swallowed her pride, told him she was ready to travel back to Wetherby.*

Then this morning she was surprised when he showed up at the train station to bid her Godspeed, and also to pay for her ticket.

"I'm the one who is making you take this journey so it's just right that I should pay for it."

Much as Charlie hadn't wanted to be beholden to him or anyone else, she knew that having extra money would come in handy especially given that she had no idea of the kind of reception she would receive at her father's house. The extra money meant that if they turned her away without listening to her, she could take a room at one of the local inns and then travel back to Manchester tomorrow.

Now here she was, and she took a deep breath and approached the large door, her battered small wooden suitcase in her hand. She used the brass knocker and the door was opened by a middle-aged female servant who gave her a curious smile. "Yes? How may I help you?" The woman looked over Charlie's shoulder. "Did you walk all the way from wherever it is that you came from?"

Charlie shook her head, "No, I just arrived from Manchester and took a carriage but dismissed it at the gate and walked the rest of the way." She didn't want to let the woman know that she had dismissed the carriage because she wanted to surprise her family, say what she had to and then leave before they could gather their senses to attack her verbally or even physically. "Now I wish that I had asked the coachman to wait for me."

"Who are you and what is it you seek on such a cold and wet day?"

"My name is Charlotte Weston and I grew up here. Where is everyone?" She asked fearfully, expecting that at any moment her father or stepmother or even half siblings would hear her voice, rush to the door and chase her away.

"The master, the mistress and the children all travelled to London for Christmas and won't be back until the New Year. They received a message that required them to travel urgently and they left just yesterday but didn't inform me that any visitors were expected. Are you sure they are expecting you?"

"I'm Mr. Weston's oldest child, and no, they weren't expecting me. I've been away from this place for a long while and decided to come and see how they are doing. Perhaps I should go and come back in the New Year," she felt relieved that her family wasn't at home. Paul would have to understand that she had at least showed up here with the intention of making things right.

"No, Miss Weston," the servant said. "Please come in out of the cold. May I take your luggage?"

"It isn't heavy, and I don't want to get you into any kind of trouble with my family. It would be best if I just returned to Manchester." She held onto the suitcase. She'd only brought a couple of dresses because she had no intention of staying for more than a day or two. All she had to do was see her parents and siblings, speak her mind and listen to what they had to say and then she would be on her way back to Manchester. Now that they weren't here, there was no way she would wait for them until the New Year. They might not like it if they found her here upon their return. No, she would only spend a single night and then be on her way on the morrow.

"Maybe I can spend the night here and then leave tomorrow," she said.

"I'll put your suitcase in the guest room," the servant said but Charlie shook her head.

"I don't belong here, and you should just allow me to use one of the servants' rooms behind the kitchen."

"Your father won't be pleased if he hears that I let you sleep in the servants' room when there are three empty guest rooms in this house."

Charlie laughed, "Oh my dear woman, my father will probably have your services terminated with immediate effect as soon as he finds out that you let me into the house in his absence. And as for my stepmother," Charlie shook her head not wanting to imagine the abuse that would be heaped on this poor woman's head, for her kindness. "But since I'll be gone before they return, you don't have to mention to them that I was ever here. It will be our secret forever."

The woman simply smiled as she stepped aside and let Charlie into the house. "If you'll allow me, I'll just take your suitcase and put it in the room that you'll use. You must want to look around and see the house again. It's very grand, isn't it? From the moment I set foot inside, I haven't stopped admiring everything."

"Yes," Charlie admitted, looking around at the house she'd grown up in. She was standing in the grand foyer and she could see vast changes. Everything looked so new and dazzling, and it was clear that her family was doing very well indeed. It brought a big lump to her throat to think that while she'd been suffering in the workhouse for all those years, her family had gone on with their lives and even prospered. It was like they had erased her very existence from their minds, and she felt bitterness rising up again. But she quashed the feelings because that wasn't the reason she was here. "How long have you worked for my family?"

"Marjory, who is the cook, and I arrived a few days ago just before your family left for London. My name is Naomi and I'm the housekeeper here."

"I expected to see more servants and people moving around the house in preparation for Christmas." When she'd lived in this house there were six servants and a governess and yet none of them had been allowed to wait on her in any way. If anything, she'd been treated worse than the lowliest of the servants.

"Your parents gave them time off until the New Year. They all travelled to be with their families but since Marjory and I were the newest and the house couldn't be left unattended, we stayed behind. That reminds me, Miss Weston, I need to let Marjory know that you're here so she can prepare dinner for you."

"Thank you," Charlie said as she stood in the grand foyer and watched Naomi walking away with her suitcase.

TERRIBLE MEMORIES

Fourteen Years Ago

"If you don't polish those wooden tiles until they shine, I'll box your ears until they ring and turn black and blue," her mother told her one spring morning.

"Mama, my knees hurt," Four-year-old Charlotte sobbed. Her little knees were bruised from kneeling for so long on the cold hard floor. She could hear her siblings playing outside because the weather was wonderful, and their laughter made her long for the freedom they had. Four-year-old Chelsea,

three-year-old Tiffany and two-year-old Albert never did any chores but spent most of their time playing while she had to polish the tiles. Like any other four-year-old, Charlie wanted to go outside and play with her siblings.

"Your knees aren't the only ones that will hurt, you insolent girl. Now polish this floor or you'll know who I am today."

Charlie polished the tiles, tears coursing down her cheeks. From time to time, her mother would come in to check on her, point out a spot she'd left out and strike her with a stick that she had in her hands. Her siblings were the ones causing her so much distress because as soon as she finished polishing one section of the foyer, they would run in with dusty shoes, slide across the floor and she was forced to do everything all over again. Finally she had enough and when Chelsea, who was just two weeks younger than she was entered the foyer, she snapped.

"Get out at once," she screamed at Chelsea, "Or I'll hit you with this rug."

"Mama," Chelsea ran screaming from the foyer. "Charlie hit me with the dirty cloth."

"What?" Her mother charged into the foyer. "How dare you delinquent child lay a hand on my princess?" She gave Charlie a resounding slap that snapped her little head back.

"Mama, I didn't hit Chelsea," Charlie screamed in pain. But her mother picked her up, shook her till her teeth rattled then flung her back on the floor.

"My children don't tell lies. You're nothing but a troublemaker, Charlie, and I will make sure your father hears of this. How dare you lay a hand on my child?"

Charlie wiped her eyes as she fell on her knees, sobbing in anguish. She cried for the little girl she'd been and who had suffered so much. She had polished this floor until her hands and knees were raw. But it was never enough and for the next six years that she'd lived in this house, she would polish this floor once a month come rain or sunshine, without any help from her siblings or the other servants. In all that time it had never once occurred to her that she was a half sibling to the others. The two weeks' age difference between her and Chelsea had never made her wonder. And yet while her half-sister had played, she had worked.

"Why?" She cried as she crawled across the foyer from one side to the other, touching every tile that she had polished. In her day the wooden tiles had shone but when she looked at them now, they had a dull lustre attesting to the fact that no one laboured over them as hard as she had done. "Why?" She finally collapsed in a corner and wept for a long time. She had been so innocent and had no idea of the crime she had supposedly committed by being born alive. At the time she had no idea that the woman she thought of as her mother was her stepmother. It had broken her little heart to see how her siblings were favoured while she was tormented day and night. Why hadn't her own father showed her any mercy?

It was a while later that Charlie wiped her tears and sat up in the foyer. Still on her knees she crawled from the grand foyer and entered the great hall, stopping at the door and looking into the large room. Her family had entertained vastly because her stepmother loved to show off that they were wealthy. In days gone by this room would be brightly lit, there would be musicians playing and clinking glasses as people made merry. Her stepmother wouldn't spare any expenses and the room would be filled with the sweet scent of flowers especially in spring and summer. Many people had yearned to be invited into this house because of the dazzling great hall and even now Charlie could see that it was still a spectacular room. She was taken back in time again.

The ball was in full swing and there were many distinguished guests present. Charlie had overheard from one of the servants that her parents were entertaining the new Duke of Yorkshire who had just returned from Europe where he'd been living for many years. A distant descendant of the House of Stuart, his father and other relatives had gone to live abroad when the House of Stuart had become extinct after the death of Cardinal Henry Benedict Stuart. Now the gentleman had returned to try and reclaim the title and her stepmother was in raptures over the thought of having a connection with nobility. All this was whispered by the servants in the kitchen as they bustled around making preparations for the great spring ball.

Charlie had hidden in the nursery upstairs, pressing her face to the window to see all the fancy carriages as they came down the driveway and discharged their occupants at the front door. She dreamed of one day owning such fancy clothes and being transported in the beautiful carriages. Then one of the servants came in and found her.

"What are you doing in here, Charlie?"

"Miss Hannah, see the beautiful carriages and the people wearing such nice clothes and hats. I wish I had pretty dresses to wear like Chelsea."

"Well, maybe one day you'll have them. Shall I tell you a secret?"

Charlie nodded.

"There is a duke and even a duchess present."

To five-year-old Charlie, a duke sounded like a wonderful and amazing being. She'd overheard the governess reading fairy tales to her five siblings. In the stories she told, there were grand dukes and their duchesses who rode in fancy carriages and wore golden cloaks.

"I wish I could see the duke and duchess," she said longingly.

"Your sister is downstairs, why don't you go and stand next to her? Mrs. Kenton allowed her to hide behind one of the drapes and watch whatever was going on and see all those well-dressed people. But make sure you don't get into any trouble or your Mama will be very vexed. Go down to your sister and remember what I said. Don't get into any trouble. Go out through the kitchen door and then sneak in through one of the windows in the foyer."

Charlie needed no second bidding and just as the maid had said, she found her sister hiding behind one of the large drapes in the grand foyer.

"Charlie, do you want to see the guests?" Chelsea whispered and she nodded. Their parents had forbidden them from ever entering the great hall whenever there were visitors present but Charlie couldn't help being curious. She really wanted to see what a duke looked like and she followed her sister, not aware of the malicious glint in her eyes. There was a male servant standing at the entrance leading from the foyer to the great hall and much as Chelsea begged, he refused to let them through.

"Your parents said that none of you should enter the great hall. Now run along and play," he'd shooed them away.

"Let's just go back to the nursery and watch the visitors who are still coming," Charlie said, feeling quite disappointed. But she didn't want to get into trouble with her father. "They won't let us in, and Papa will be cross if he finds us out here."

"You're such a little coward," Chelsea taunted.

"I'm not a coward," Charlie said with false bravado.

"Oh, but you are," Chelsea teased. "Even little Trevor is braver than you," Chelsea referred to their youngest sibling who was just a few months old and learning to crawl. "Everyone will laugh at the coward called Charlie. Charlie the coward," Chelsea chanted unkindly.

"Shut up, I'm not a coward."

"Then show everyone that you're not the cowardly coward that you are."

"How?"

"Go and enter the great hall and greet the duke," Chelsea dared her.

Mention of the duke is what did it for Charlie. "But Mr. Miles won't let us into the hall," she pointed at the servant who was staring at them menacingly.

"Use the window and slip in. We can hide behind the drapes until the duke passes by and then greet him. That's how I'll know that you're not a coward. Come." Charlie foolishly followed Chelsea out to the lawn and then they slipped in through one of the large open windows. Since it was toward the end of spring all the windows were wide open to let in as much air as possible since the great hall was crowded.

Charlie was scared when she found herself inside the forbidden room, so she quickly slipped behind one of the drapes. There were grownups everywhere and she knew that if her parents saw her, she would be in so much trouble. Just as she was thinking about slipping out through the window to safety, she felt someone shove her forward. Unfortunately, someone was just walking toward her carrying a tall glass with red wine. She felt another shove and she sprawled right in front of the adult, startling him such that his hand jerked, and he spilled a good amount of the red wine down the front of his shirt. Her heart sank when she realised what had happened.

"Oh confound it! This little imp has ruined my shirt," the man's voice was high pitched, and he shouted in anger. Handing his half-empty glass to a passing servant, he reached down and hauled Charlie to her feet. "Who are you and what are you doing here?"

"I'm sorry," Charlie was visibly trembling and praying that the man would put her down so she could dart away. But he was so angry and made sure that everyone knew of it.

"This insolent child has ruined my expensive silk shirt," he told anyone who cared to listen. Charlie heard people's snickers, which only made the man angrier. She had no idea that the very person who was shaking her was the duke she had so longed to see. There were murmurs all around and Charlie prayed for the ground to open up and swallow her when her father stepped forward, profusely apologizing to the duke but giving her the evil eye.

Charlie moaned as she recalled the beating her father had meted out in his study where he'd dragged her to from the great hall.

"You have embarrassed me in front of my guests," *and the lashes had seemed to go on forever until* *she lost consciousness.*

She closed her eyes as huge sobs wracked her slender frame, feeling the lashes landing on her back as they had fourteen years ago. She'd been ill for a whole week and it was one of the servants who had taken pity and bathed the welts with warm salty water. But even though the bruises had eventually healed, she still had the scars on her back from the beating.

"The poor girl will make herself ill, Naomi," Marjory whispered. They could hear the broken sobs coming from the great hall. "I don't want to imagine what terrible things she must be remembering."

"It's so heartbreaking," Naomi agreed. "But we can only be here to provide nourishment and leave her alone. This is her father's house and she has been away for a long time, so it's just natural for her to have painful memories. She will soon calm down and then we can serve her dinner. I'll put hot water in the pitcher in readiness for when she needs it for her bath, for I'm sure she will be feeling grimy."

"It's all too sad."

Naomi nodded, "I agree but what can we do?"

TWO DAYS TO CHRISTMAS

It had been a terrible night for her, and Charlie felt drained. Her face was puffy from all the weeping she'd done the previous day and her throat hurt. She couldn't recall the last time she had cried so much.

"I can't do this," she shook her head as she lay in bed. Last evening, Naomi had picked her up from the great hall, half carrying and half dragging her up the stairs to one of the smaller guest rooms. She had asked about her old room in the attic and was informed that it was now used as storage space.

She had collapsed on the bed and Naomi had forcefully fed her some chicken broth and a hot bun. She'd been too weak to even raise a spoon to her lips. The memories were too painful, and she didn't think she could go through another heart-wrenching day in this house. It was as though everything was happening like it had back then.

"I have to get away," she dragged her weary body out of bed and put on clean clothes. After quickly packing her suitcase which Naomi had unpacked, she made sure nothing of hers was left in the room. The last thing she wanted was for Naomi and Marjory to get into trouble with her parents when they returned. It was all for the best that she leave today. No one need know she had even been here. Wishing she could shut her eyes and just float out of the house without glimpsing any of the other rooms where she'd suffered, she walked out of the guest room and to the stairs, then put her hand to the balustrade. She was ready to go down the stairs and leave this house forever, never to return.

"Are you leaving so soon?" Naomi's voice floated up from the bottom of the stairs, startling her. Charlie jerked, the wooden suitcase slipped from her hands and she watched in dismay as it tumbled down the stairs till it crashed at the bottom, splitting into two pieces because it was old. She had bought it at a thrift store, and she stared at her scanty belongings which had scattered in different directions. "I'm sorry, I didn't mean to startle you," Naomi gathered the scattered items and tried to put them back into the suitcase and put the lid back on, but it was a futile attempt. "This is ruined. But I don't understand why you're leaving so soon, Miss Weston."

"I told you that I would only spend the night since my parents aren't here. It's not possible for me to stay here until the New Year because they weren't expecting me, and I wouldn't want you to get into any kind of trouble with them."

"It's a pity since this is your father's house and you should feel free here. But I also must point out to you that there are no trains running today on account of the bad weather. The only other means of conveyance is by stagecoach and those are not as safe as they used to be before. With the coming of the trains, fewer stagecoaches are running and this means they are easy targets for highwaymen and bandits. You would be in a lot of trouble especially if you had to get stuck at an inn along the way in the middle of nowhere. Miss Weston, I can't let you leave in this terrible weather."

"But I don't want to stay here," Charlie suddenly felt uneasy as though there were someone else in the house watching her. "Where is Mrs. Marjory?"

"She's in the kitchen, why?" Naomi's eyes narrowed when she saw Charlie's eyes darting all over the place as if searching for something.

"I don't know, but I just got a funny feeling as if someone is watching us," she shivered then smiled sheepishly at the woman's raised eyebrows. "Maybe this house is getting to me. I really need to get out of here and back to Manchester. Maybe I'll take my chances with the stagecoach."

"Even those may not be willing to take you on in this poor weather. Why don't you wait until tomorrow? Perhaps the weather will have cleared then and once again be safe for travels."

"But tomorrow is Christmas Eve."

"Of course, it is, and just so you know, if the weather permits, the trains will resume on schedule and you can then travel back to Manchester. But for now, why don't you go to the dining hall while I carry your belongings back to the room upstairs. I'll bring you some breakfast, and then you'll feel better after you've eaten something."

Charlie nodded and watched as the woman tied all her belongings in an old scarf and tossed it over her shoulder. With her other hand she picked up the two useless pieces of the suitcase and started on her way up. "Go on, just go and make yourself comfortable. I'll be with you in a short while."

Charlie walked to the dining room and stopped at the doorway. This was another room that had been forbidden to her. She'd been relegated to taking her meals in the kitchen with the other servants and the only time she was ever allowed in here was when she had turned eight and was expected to serve the family. Practically a slave in her own father's house!

Ten Years Ago

Charlie was eight when she finally gathered the courage to ask her mother why she wasn't allowed to take meals in the dining room with the rest of the family.

"You insolent child," her mother had screamed at her. "You forget your place in this house. Those who are allowed to sit in the dining room are family and not just every riffraff is allowed in."

"Mama aren't I a part of this family?" Charlie was shocked at the ugly words from her mother's lips. "I thought I was Papa's eldest child."

And her efforts were rewarded with a resounding slap as she was pushed out of the dining room by her sisters while her father looked up from his newspaper. A disinterested glance in her direction was all he afforded her before he returned to his reading.

A few days later she was compelled to carry a steaming pot of soup to the dining room and her brother Willis tripped her. She stumbled and the pot shook, scalding her little hands and she dropped the porcelain pot which cracked and all the soup poured on the floor. Her stepmother had made her *lick the soup from the floor while her half siblings laughed.*

"You wanted to sit at the dining table with the rest of the family, now eat whatever it is that was supposed to be served. Go on," her stepmother pressed her face to the floor. Charlie begged her father to save her but all he did was to get up and actually step over her on his way out, never once saying a word.

"It's too much," Charlie fell on her knees and sobbed in anguish, feeling like her head was about to burst. It was Naomi who found her on the floor as she brought her breakfast in a few minutes later.

"Oh Child," the woman exclaimed, setting the tray on the table and coming around to help her up. "You carry so much pain and it's time to let it go. You will make yourself ill with so much weeping."

"It's too painful," Charlie allowed herself to be seated on one of the plush chairs. She'd never sat on any of the chairs at the dining table and even now she felt afraid that her parents or siblings would come in and then she would be in trouble. "I'm not allowed to sit here."

"Why do you say that?" Naomi gently soothed. "This is where the family takes all their meals and as part of them it's only fitting that you do so as well."

"No, you don't understand. If my parents find me sitting at the dining table there will be a lot of trouble, not only for me but for you as well. My place is in the kitchen," she tried to rise up, but the older woman put a restraining hand on her shoulder.

"There's no one else in this house save for Marjory and me, and we won't be telling your folks that you sat at the dining table to take your meals. Now, eat something because yesterday you barely touched what we had prepared for you. I don't like seeing you like this and just wish that you would let your pain go."

"How do I do that when I've carried it for so many years? Mrs. Naomi, you don't know what it was like growing up in this house with parents who hated me and siblings who always found a way of getting me into trouble. All five of my siblings are younger than me but they made my life a living hell," she shook her head. "How do you expect me to let all that go?"

"You can't do it in your own strength, Miss Weston. Ask the Lord to help you…"

"Stop," Charlie covered her ears with her hands. "That Lord that you speak of never helped me before and I don't believe in His existence anyway. Why would He let me go through all that suffering if He really cared?"

"Miss Weston, no one can ever imagine what you went through. That pain has filled your heart and pushed out all your awareness of God. But I know that deep down in your heart you still believe in Him. Or else you wouldn't be so angry at Him. You can't be angry at someone Who doesn't exist. Just give Him your pain, for He promised to bear it for you."

"Please leave me alone," Charlie begged. "Just let me be."

"I'll be in the kitchen if you need anything."

"Thank you."

For the sake of gaining strength, Charlie forced herself to eat the toast, ham and eggs that Mrs. Naomi had brought her and drank a cup of tea. When she was done, she moved to the window and looked out. Just as Mrs. Naomi had said, it was snowing heavily, and the whole place was white. No one would dare venture out in this weather and she knew that she was stuck here for another day.

She cleared the table and carried the dishes to the kitchen, which was empty. She washed them at the large sink, tears coursing down her face as she remembered the hard times she'd endured in this kitchen. Yet this had also been a place of refuge sometimes depending on which servant was working in the kitchen at the time. Some of the servants would hide her from her stepmother's wrath and also feed her some titbits from the master's table. But one or two of the other servants had also made her life difficult. They were her stepmother's spies and would always report on her.

When the dishes were all done, she arranged them neatly on the counter and went out. As she walked out of the kitchen, her feet seemed to have a mind of their own and she passed through the great hall, surprised that she no longer felt so much pain about entering into this room. What she didn't realise was that her heart was slowly healing with all the weeping that she was doing. So she walked through the great hall and into the foyer where she passed the cloakroom where she paused and touched the door. It was a large room and could have fitted a small size cot.

Nine Years Ago

Charlie had just turned nine years old and the vicar had come visiting. As usual, cloaks, stoles, scarves and hats were placed in the cloakroom and handed back to their owners when they were ready to depart. Usually there was a servant who took care of the visitors' property while they were in the house but on that particular day, Charlie had been polishing the foyer floor when the vicar called in to visit her mother.

After receiving his cloak and stole, the servant told Charlie to watch the door while he went to get a drink of water. The child was relieved at having not been told to get close to the cloakroom because she was terrified of entering it. From when she was four years old, Charlie had learnt to steer clear of the cloakroom because more than once her siblings had locked her in there and she'd nearly suffocated but for a servant finding out what was going on and saving her.

Once the servant had left her post, Charlie's stepmother called out and asked her to find a scarf which she'd supposedly left in the cloakroom. Heart in mouth, the child entered the dreaded room and searched all over but couldn't find the scarf and informed her stepmother.

"Go to the kitchen and help with the lunch preparation," she was told and did as bid.

But when it was time for the vicar to leave, his beautiful and very expensive stole was nowhere to be found.

"Charlie was holding it," seven-year-old Tiffany who was her second sister said. "I saw her putting it around her neck, Mama."

"That's not true, Mama," Charlie trembled at the ugly expression on her mother's face. "I only touched it to move it out of the way as I was searching for your scarf. I didn't take it out of the cloakroom, Mama. Please believe me."

"Mama," Chelsea gave her a malicious look, "I saw Charlie with my own two eyes. She took the stole and carried it to her room when she thought no one was watching her."

Her mother sent two servants to the attic where she slept, and they turned it upside down but didn't find the stole.

"You will produce the stole," her mother said. "Or your father will deal with you when he returns. You're a thief, Charlie, and it's true that a viper begets a viper. A thief's child also becomes a thief, and you're nothing more than a troublemaker."

Charlie looked to the vicar, the man of God who always preached about love and understanding. She was hoping he would intervene, but he glared angrily at her and she recalled one of the sermons he'd preached not too long ago.

"Material things don't matter, and we should never place too much value on them. The important thing for Christians is to love one another and not see material things as being of more importance than good relations."

She looked at him once again and wondered where the love he had preached so loudly from the pulpit was.

"Mrs. Weston," the vicar said instead, "This child needs to be disciplined and taught that stealing is a sin, and if she doesn't repent then she will go to hell. Don't tolerate a thief in your midst for she will teach the other children all her bad habits. Spare not the rod and spoil not the child," he cried out.

Her mother slapped her and demanded that she bring back the stole. And just as she was about to give Charlie another blow, a servant entered the foyer carrying the stole that was being looked for.

"Mrs. Weston, is this what you seek?" he asked, looking at Charlie who was on the floor and holding her stinging cheek, tears coursing down her face. There was pity in his eyes. "Vicar Thomas, you dropped your stole on the lawn when you alighted from your carriage. I picked it up and intended to bring it inside but one of the stable boys called me to help with one of the mares which was foaling. I kept it with me until we were done," he held it out to the vicar.

Charlie leaned her head tiredly against the cloakroom door and closed her eyes. Her mother and sisters hadn't apologized for the gross mistake, and the damage was done. She'd been branded as a thief even though she was innocent of what she'd been accused of. And the vicar had also not said a word but simply taken his stole, his face red with embarrassment and left the house in a hurry. From that day, she stopped believing in anything that was preached from the pulpit and even when she was forced to accompany the family to church, she never went close to the vicar who had declared her a thief and relegated her to the fires of hell when she'd been innocent.

A painful tightness gripped Charlie's throat as she approached the music and dancing room. From when she was very little, she'd loved music and dancing. But the governesses and tutor never once let her into the room while her siblings were having their lessons. And once Charlie had left home after finding out that her birth mother had died just three days after she was born, the girl had wept for all her broken dreams that would never be realised.

She liked to believe that had her mother had the chance to live, she would have fled the house of torture and taken Charlie with her. Perhaps they would have suffered but they would have been together, and her special talent would have been discovered. All Charlie had to do was listen to a piece of music and then she could play it from memory.

"Maybe if I learn to play well, Papa will be proud of me," the little girl had thought. She was ten at the time and her father completely ignored her existence and she was starved for his affection. She always looked on longingly when he carried her siblings on his shoulders, and she wished he would do the same for her. But he would simply glare at her and then ignore her as if she weren't even present.

Many times, Charlie had cried herself to sleep and always told herself that her father was a wealthy and kind man who had travelled to a distant land and left her with these people. She would imagine him returning to take her away from this place and to a beautiful manor somewhere. There she would find a beautiful bedchamber with everything she had ever desired. But most of all she would be with her father who would laugh with her, carry her on his shoulders and tell her every day that she was beautiful and he loved her.

She sighed at her childish dreams and desires. Her stepmother never allowed her into the nursery for any lessons, but she would often steal Chelsea and Tiffany's school slates and do their homework for them. That was how she managed to get the little education she had. But even though her sisters knew that she did their homework and correctly, they never once thanked her and if anything, they only became more hostile toward her. They taught the little boys to also despise Charlie and she had no friend among her siblings. Little did she know that her stepmother and half siblings were jealous of not only her intelligence and talents but her beauty as well. It was as though they were out to crush her spirit and reduce her to nothing.

Music was in her blood and as Charlie walked up to the old piano and uncovered it, tears coursed down her face. She uncovered it and her fingers ran lovingly over the tuneless keys. It was obvious that it hadn't been tuned or played for a while from the dust that had gathered between the keys and on the lid. The first time she knew that she could play was when she was five and had been told to dust the piano. She'd sat down on this very same old stool, her legs hanging in the air and when she touched the keys it was as though she'd been transported into another world. She had played her little heart out, not knowing that her stepmother had heard and come to the door.

And Charlie recalled the last time she had played the piano and once again she found herself gasping for breath. She could hear the little girl she had been sobbing in pain when her stepmother had come into the music room and found her playing.

"You think you're so smart and clever," she had hissed and brought the lid crashing down hard. And even now, eight years later, Charlie gasped, remembering the pain she had felt as her right middle finger and left ring finger were broken by the impact of the lid on her small hands.

She raised both hands and looked at her disfigured digits. She couldn't bend either finger because no one had bothered to get her any treatment. Just a few days after that horrible incident, her father had hauled her out of the house and tossed her into a carriage. And she had been weeping as her stepmother and half siblings stood on the front porch smiling broadly. The carriage ride had been endless and because of the pain she was feeling from her broken fingers, the child had slipped in and out of consciousness. When she finally regained consciousness, it was days later, and she was in a strange dark room.

"What did I ever do to deserve all this," Charlie bent her head and let the tears fall on the ivory and ebony keys. Maybe if her mother had lived, she would have become one of England's greatest pianists. But now she would never know because her fingers were disfigured, and the music had gone out of her soul and heart.

Then rage filled her, and she rose up, bringing the lid crashing down and she struck it with her fists. These people had stolen her childhood and her dreams, and they didn't deserve to be forgiven. Paul was asking too much of her, and she didn't think she could do it. She loved him but if this was the price she had to pay, then she no longer wanted to be with him. Paul expected too much of her, but she wasn't ready to let go. No, someone had to pay for all the pain and humiliation she had suffered for eighteen years. She had been treated shamefully by everyone, and the worst person of all was her father, the man who should have protected her but had instead turned a blind eye to all her suffering.

What had led her to discover that her stepmother wasn't her birth mother was when she had been cleaning her father's study one day. She was ten years old at the time and it was just two days before the incident in which her fingers had been mutilated. Her father had walked into the study, and because she didn't want to get into trouble, she crawled under his massive table and sat there trembling. Her stepmother walked in a few minutes later and a quarrel ensued.

"You are a worthless man, Archibald. How could you betray me with that filthy servant? Do you know that she came and told me that you had forced yourself on her? What kind of a man are

you, or were you carrying on with her behind my back?"

"Not now, Marigold," her father said in a harsh voice. "And keep your voice down. Do you want all the servants to hear you?"

"I don't care if they hear me because I want them to know what kind of man you are. And now I am beginning to believe that Stacy might have been right after all. You followed her to her room in the servants' wing and did what you did. Why did you allow her to carry that accursed child at all?"

"There was no way I could get rid of Stacy because she would have gone out there and told everyone," Charlie frowned at the fear in her father's voice. "And the child was innocent."

"You should have put that child in a foundling home and then none of this would have ever come up. Do you know that the servants have been telling everyone that we are mistreating Charlotte? And just the other day, Mrs. Haines the leader of the Mothers' Union in church had the audacity to ask me where my Christian charity was. She

claimed that they were thinking about relieving me of my post as the secretary of the Union. What shame is that upon me? I told you to get rid of Charlotte because she isn't my child but you refused. Now see what all this has brought."

"What did you want me to do, Marigold? Stacy was dead and the child had nowhere else to go."

"You should have taken her to the orphanage. If that girl hadn't died three days after giving birth to Charlotte, I would have sent them both away and then none of this shame and humiliation would have come upon you. This is all your fault, Archibald, and I expect you to make things right or I will take my children and return to my father's estate. You can then choose to force yourself on one of the other servants and turn them into your wife and make her care for that baseborn child of yours."

That was the day that she had finally known the truth about her birth mother and understood why Mrs. Marigold Weston, who she'd always thought of as her mother, had loathed her with a passion.

Falling on her knees, Charlie crawled under the piano and raised her knees. She put her head on them and wept some more. It was a miracle that her life had been preserved and spared. It was also a miracle that her virtue had been spared. Because right from the moment she had been tossed into the workhouse, there were those who had sought to degrade her and forcefully take her virtue away. They never cared that she was just a child and had sought to hurt her in the worst way possible. But something always happened to prevent those men from carrying out their evil deeds on her body.

And then Ragland had become her friend and protector and taught her how to fight and defend herself, or to hide. The day she had broken someone's nose is the day everyone had begun fearing her, even calling her the offspring of the devil. But they had left her alone after that until she had turned seventeen and been sent out of the workhouse just two days before her eighteenth birthday.

"No, I can't forgive," she hissed. One day they would all pay for their crimes against her, from her father to the master and matrons in the workhouse, her stepmother and half siblings. They would pay, to the very last person.

BEING MADE WHOLE

It was very early in the morning on Christmas Eve. Charlie was feeling feverish and she knew that it was because the previous day she had spent hours on the cold floor in the music room. From there she had moved to the sewing room, which was now empty, recalling all the fancy clothes she had sewed for her family and even her stepmother's friends. Yet not once had she ever had a new dress. All the clothes she wore had been her stepmother's old and frayed ones that should have just been burnt or tossed out.

But the sewing room had also been one of the other places, apart from the kitchen where she had found some respite. As she had recalled all the years of stitching and pricking her little fingers until she bled, the pain of being nothing more than a slave in her father's house had left her weak and she felt like all strength was gone from her.

"Let me die now," she had sobbed. It was Mrs. Marjory who had found her shivering on the sewing room floor and carried her to bed, tucking her in. The woman had then lit a small fire in the room and brought in hot stones which she wrapped in some cloth and placed at Charlie's feet. But even with two quilts covering her and the fire in the room, Charlie still felt so cold and was delirious, begging for death to come and take her away from all the pain.

"Just take my life," she sobbed. "Let me die right now so I can finally rest," she prayed as her eyes closed in fitful sleep.

Suddenly Charlie was a ten-year-old again standing in the corner of the workhouse clutching a tattered book in her hands. It was her one and only precious possession because it was the first gift she had ever received with love. The book had been given to her by one of the older women in the workhouse who had taken her in as soon as she was dumped there by her father. But sadly, Mrs. Amber Hawke had only lived for a month after Charlie's arrival, her broken body full of sores and ravaged by a debilitating disease. Though Charlie couldn't read very well at the time, the book had given her a lot of comfort, at least at first.

"This book will give you life," Mrs. Hawke had told her. "Treasure it and never let it be far from you. You will find all of life's answers in this book."

Then the little girl looked down at the book and her face turned dark with rage as she flung it across the room, its pages scattering all over the floor.

"Lies," she screamed. "Jesus, You're a liar and a thief," she fell on her knees and sobbed. "Where is the life You promised and why did You allow Mrs. Hawke to die? She believed in You, but You lied to her. You're not to be trusted," she wept. "Get away from me and stay away from my life because I can never believe anything You say again. Keep Your Book. You're just like everyone else, cruel and mean." She cried for a long time and darkness overcame her, covering her like a thick cloak.

Charlie moaned and twitched in the bed, struggling against the darkness.

"Look up," a voice commanded but she refused. "Charlotte raise your head."

"No, leave me alone," she shouted. But then a strong force like a hand held her chin and raised her face. "Look closely," the command came again.

Charlie opened her eyes and fixed her gaze on the wall before her when she saw the silhouette of a man being whipped. As each lash fell across his back, stripping the flesh off and causing blood to pour out, He cried out and she found herself doing the same. Then she saw that all His clothes had been stripped off his body. Something heavy like a rugged tree trunk was placed over the Man's shoulder and He fell on His knees, but the whipping didn't cease. Then she saw long sharp nails being driven into the man's palms and feet and she screamed out as if the pain was hers.

"If He already paid the price for the sins of the world, do you want your family forgiven or should the wrath of God wreak revenge on them?"

"Crucify them," Charlie screamed. "They deserve to die, all of them. Don't forgive, just crucify them."

Once again deep darkness overcame her, and she lay still as one who was dead. Then the same voice that had commanded her before broke through the darkness again.

"Look!"

"No... strength...." She gasped. The same hand raised her chin again and she opened her eyes. She could see sharp arrows shooting from her hands and lips and they pierced the Man who was hanging on the rugged tree. All around Him she could see different people and their faces became clearer to her. Her father, stepmother, her five siblings, the workhouse supervisors, both male and female, all of them were either shooting sharp arrows or casting stones at the Man, striking Him and causing Him to bleed. What surprised Charlie was that not once did He raise His voice to curse or say anything bad against anyone.

"But He was wounded for our transgressions, He was bruised for our iniquities: the chastisement of our peace was upon Him; and with His stripes we are healed. All we like sheep have gone astray, we have turned everyone to his own way; and the Lord hath laid on Him the iniquity of us ALL!"

"All?" Charlie asked in a whisper.

"All of them," the voice said, and as she looked, the Man hanging on the tree cried out.

"It is finished," He bowed His head and died. And then something wonderful happened. Charlie saw all the arrows that had pierced the Man on the tree shrivelling as if they were dying with him and then they fell harmlessly to the ground. Suddenly also, a seed fell to the ground and as she watched, it began to sprout and then it grew and grew…"

"Behold Child, old things are passed away and all things have become new." Then it was as if a vile river began to flow out of her mouth. The taste was foul and she was choking on it but she kept spewing it out. It was coming from deep within her belly and she thought she would die from the violent retching. Then the foul water ceased and suddenly her mouth was filled with fresh water that was so sweet, and she drank and drank. It was as a never-ending stream and as she drank from it, her whole body began to get lighter and the darkness that had surrounded her began to

fade away until there was only bright light left. And for the first time, Charlie felt something she hadn't known in her life—deep peace.

Charlie shot up from under the quilt and looked around the bedchamber, eyes wide open. "Was that a dream or a vision?" she touched her heart and then folded both fists. All her fingers, even the disfigured ones bent easily and there was no pain. So she raised her hands and stared at them, flexing her fingers. They were straight and beautiful, and she gasped. She had to be dreaming because her fingers were disfigured forever.

"What is happening to me?" She slowly got out of bed. The lamp was burning brightly, and she couldn't recall lighting it. The whole room was flooded with light. Laughter bubbled from within her. It was such a freeing emotion that she gave in to it, laughing softly until she fell on her knees with tears coursing down her cheeks. Yet these were no longer tears of pain and rage, but she felt as though she was being washed clean.

"Forgive them Father," she found herself saying. "Forgive them all, every last one of them, for they knew not what they were doing. And forgive me too."

Archibald Weston suddenly sat up in bed. "What is it?" his wife Marigold had been disturbed by her husband's restlessness throughout the night. "Can't you sleep anymore?"

"I don't know what it is, but we have to go back home."

"It's very early in the morning on Christmas Day," Marigold cried out. "Why do you want us to go back home? Didn't you promise that we would stay in London until the New Year, Archibald? You promised us a good break this Christmas. What is happening?"

Archibald Weston got out of bed. He was a tall and slender man with green eyes and dark hair. He was still handsome, but grooves lined his face like someone who was deeply anxious. He looked down at his wife of twenty years and saw the scowl on her face. For as long as he could recall, she was always angry, and for the first time in his life, he acknowledged that he was the cause of it all.

Marigold was still a pretty woman, but anger had distorted her classic features and she had a permanent frown on her face. When he'd first met and fallen in love with her, her beauty had struck him. They had been so full of love and hope for the future. At the time of meeting and subsequent marriage, Marigold's father was a cobbler and owned a prosperous shoe store which he'd left to Archie upon his death just a year after their marriage. Her mother and brothers still lived on their small estate in York.

Because of the grief of losing her father within a year of her marriage, Marigold had lost two pregnancies. The doctor had warned her that she would have to wait for a few years before conceiving again or else she might lose her life. Her pain and bitterness had made their once happy marriage a strenuous one, and in a fit of rage, Archie had grabbed his chambermaid and forced her to lie with him.

"If my wife can't have children then I might as well get one in any way that I can," he'd told the sobbing young girl who was only fourteen at the time. Her body was broken but he didn't care at the time and life had never been the same for them again.

"Marigold," Archie looked at his wife and knelt down beside the bed. "I'm so sorry for the terrible things that I did in the past and for putting you through so much pain and anguish. Please forgive me."

Marigold stared at her husband who had never once said sorry for anything. His eyes were shimmering with unshed tears and she saw genuine brokenness and remorse in them. Something broke within her too.

"Oh Archie," she burst into tears. "Please forgive me for not being the woman you hoped that I would be."

"It's easy to forgive because I love you so much. I broke our vows and did terrible things, and may God forgive me too."

Marigold started sobbing hard.

"What is it, my love?"

"Archie, we have to find…."

"No, don't mention her name," he cried out hoarsely. "My heart can't take it."

"We were so wrong, but we can't ignore that we wanted to destroy an innocent child's life."

"May God forgive us," he wept.

"You have to find Charlotte and bring her back home," Marigold cried. "I can't live with the guilt anymore, it's killing me."

"Immediately the holidays are over, I'll go to the workhouse and bring her home."

A NEW DAY

She felt new, and as she gathered everything of hers and stuffed them into an old carpetbag that Mrs. Naomi had found from somewhere, Charlie knew that her life would never be the same again. She was going back to Manchester to find the man she loved and who had led her to this point in her life. "I'm finally free," she said, a beautiful smile on her face.

While she knew that the memories would continue to resurface from time to time, she was confident that she now had the strength to overcome them and not allow bitterness to take over her soul and heart again.

"Thank You, Jesus," she looked heavenward and smiled. "It's Your birthday today, and this is the greatest and best gift that You have bestowed upon me. Your salvation has set me free and I am so full of joy." Now she understood what Paul had tried to tell her.

"When you finally get to the place where you can forgive everyone who has hurt you then and only then will you experience the peace that passes all human understanding. And your life will never remain the same again. It will be as though everything is new again."

Charlie laughed out loud, "Oh Paul, I love you so much and can't wait to see you again." It was true, and she ran to the window to look outside. Everything looked new, and she couldn't wait to get out into the world and live again.

She walked out of the room with her luggage. It was a bright day and the sun was shining, though it was not yet even seven in the morning. Leaving the carpetbag in the grand foyer, Charlie went to share Christmas greetings with the two women who had taken care of her in her darkest hours.

"You look really happy," Mrs. Naomi was the first to see her as soon as she entered the kitchen. She could smell the delicious aromas of gingerbread and roasting fowl. She also smelled a pie and regretted that she wouldn't be around for lunch. Hopefully if she caught the earliest train she would be in Manchester by mid-afternoon. Then she could share Christmas Day supper with Mrs. Kincaid and hopefully Paul, if she could find him.

"Oh Mrs. Naomi, I feel so free and happy," she raised her hands in the air and twirled around. "See, my fingers are healed, and I am whole again," she rubbed her heart. "There's something so different inside here. It's a beautiful Christmas Day, and I have a feeling that everything is going to be so wonderful from now on."

"The Lord has taken away your wounded and bruised heart and given you a new one. Now you are a new person, Miss Weston."

"Thank you for taking such good care of me, and I pray that you don't get into any trouble with my parents. I have to go back to Manchester because there's someone waiting for me there."

"Won't you wait for your parents to return?"

Charlie shook her head, "If I might impose on you for the last time for a cup of tea and a pie before I leave for the railway station."

"Of course, of course," Mrs. Marigold bustled around. "Go and sit in the dining room and I'll bring you breakfast right away. And I'll also pack something for you to eat on your journey."

But as Charlie sat at the dining table taking her breakfast, she felt compelled to write letters to all the members of her family. She picked up her cup of tea and walked to her father's study. It was the one room she hadn't entered in in the past two days, and she felt deep sadness within. Nothing had changed from the last time she could recall when she had found out the truth about her mother, but she refused to let the painful memories resurface.

"Jesus took all our sins and they were nailed to the Cross with Him," she murmured as she sat in her father's chair. She opened the top drawer and pulled out an inkwell, a stylus pen and paper and wrote seven letters.

"We have to hurry," Archibald urged the carriage driver.

"Why are you in such a hurry, my Love?" Marigold asked. She was smiling and knew that her children were looking at her oddly.

"I don't know, but I feel that we need to get home very soon."

Charlie stepped out of the house, her luggage in her hand. It was about a mile's walk to the railway station and the whole world looked beautiful this morning. "Merry Christmas," she shouted to no one in particular. The seven letters were all in Naomi's keeping and the woman had promised that as soon as her family returned, she would hand them over.

Then Charlie closed the door behind her and stood on the porch for what she felt was the last time. She was walking away without any bitterness and her letters said it all. But she didn't think she would be returning this way ever again. Before she could walk down the steps, she became aware of a rattling sound and when she looked up, saw a carriage coming up the driveway. As it drew closer, she wondered who the visitors were. Then it stopped and the door opened and the first person who stepped out was her father.

Her heart began to pound because she had no idea what kind of reception they would give her. Why had they returned so suddenly, she thought? Had the servants sent them telegrams to inform them of her presence? They should have stayed in London until she got away. But she had done what she needed to do and no matter what happened or how they received her, she was walking out of this house as a free woman. All the shackles and heavy burdens had been left at the foot of the Cross of Jesus. She would never pick them up again for they were all gone.

After her father came her stepmother then siblings in order of their ages, Chelsea, Tiffany, Albert, William and lastly Trevor. They all stood there looking at her as she did the same to them.

Eight years was a long time and Charlie laughed inwardly because she hadn't thought of her siblings as grown up. Yet here they were. There was silence for a long while and even the birds stopped chirping as they flew from tree to tree. It was as though all of nature was holding its breath to see the outcome of this meeting.

It was Charlie who finally broke the silence as she moved forward, her bag in her hand. She came down the steps and then stood at a respectful distance from her family. Old habits die hard and she wasn't sure that someone wouldn't lash out at her.

"Father, Mother, I came to ask for your forgiveness."

"What?" Marigold whispered in a choked voice.

"Please forgive my mother for her sins that made her bring me into this world to hurt you. And please forgive me, too, for not being the kind of daughter you needed or deserved." Her parents gasped audibly as Charlie smiled at them. "And I forgive you too, for everything," she turned to look at the house. "For so long this house was my prison both physically and also in my mind, and I hope you don't mind that I came back here to make my peace with you all." She looked at her siblings. "Chelsea, Tiffany, Albert, William and Trevor, please forgive me also for not being the older sister you deserved."

Chelsea put a hand to her heart and a sob broke through her lips.

But Charlie wasn't done yet. "I forgive you, too. That's all I came to say. Everything else that was in my heart is in the letters that I wrote and left with Mrs. Naomi. She will give them to you after I have left. Now I must be on my way back to where I came from."

That was when Archibald moved. He couldn't believe that his daughter was here and there was no bitterness on her face or in her voice. All the way from London, he'd thought about searching for her, but he was also filled with dread about how she would respond to him. He'd thrown his daughter away and never once acknowledged her for eighteen years.

"Wait," he said as she walked past them. "Charlotte," he raised his hand and she shrank back out of instinct for survival. She dropped her bag and raised both hands with a cry, as if to ward off the blows she expected to land.

Mr. Weston's hands dropped, and he clutched at his heart, feeling such deep anguish that it nearly brought him to his knees. "I wasn't going to strike you," he choked out.

"Charlotte," her stepmother seemed nervous, but Charlie was still very wary of them all. "We came back from London because we felt the urge to return in haste. We had no idea that we would find you here."

"Please don't be angry with Mrs. Naomi and Mrs. Marigold for letting me into the house in your absence. But I needed to come and make my peace and now I will be on my way."

"Charlie," her father's voice was begging. "Can you ever forgive me for what I did to you? What can I ever say to make you extend the grace of forgiveness to me? It was all my fault that your life turned out to be so terrible. Please forgive me, my child!"

Charlie thought she was dreaming. Never had she imagined seeing her father looking so broken up and her stepmother too. This was a new beginning for all of them and she had to take the first step, but her feet felt like they were too heavy to move. So, her father moved and she was shaking as she watched him coming closer. He reached out his arms and embraced her and held her close

"My child, my firstborn," he cried, tears coursing down his cheeks. "Charlie, please forgive me, forgive us all."

"Oh Papa," Charlie finally put her arms around her father, and they wept for a long while.

The door opened but the two were still weeping in each other's arms. "You did it,

Charlie," she thought she heard Paul's voice saying. "That's my girl."

"What?" She moved out of her father's arms, and when she turned around and saw Paul, she had to blink a couple of times. "I must be dreaming," she said.

He came down the steps smiling at her. "You're not dreaming, dear girl," he said and then looked at her family. "Your family, I presume?"

"Yes, this is my father, my mother, and my sisters and brothers."

"I'm happy to meet you all," Paul said with a smile as he drew closer and took Charlie's hand. "You did it, and I'm so proud of you, Charlie. You have finally made peace and now it's time to be rewarded."

"Where did you come from?" She asked, still not believing that her beloved Paul was here in Wetherby. She thought she'd left him in Manchester and that's why she'd been in haste to return. "How is it that you're here right now?"

"I've been here all the time," he said.

"But how?"

He smiled, "We boarded the same train and arrived at the same time. But I didn't want you to know I was here because I didn't want my presence to influence any decisions you were going to make."

"Where have you been then?"

"I spent most of the time in the stable, but Mrs. Naomi and Mrs. Marigold kept me appraised of everything that was happening."

"I don't understand."

"When you told me your story, I got in touch with my aunts, Mrs. Naomi and Mrs. Marigold and asked them to travel to Wetherby," Charlie noticed that the two women had come out of the house and were standing on the front porch. "They found out that your parents were travelling to London for Christmas and somehow persuaded them to put them in their employ. I wanted them to be here when you arrived so they would guide you in every way. And I'm glad to see that your heart has been healed and you are being made whole again, Charlie."

HEED THE WARNING

"Mr. and Mrs. Weston, I know that Charlie has forgiven you all and wants to build a relationship with you all."

"Yes, that's right," Charlie's father smiled at Paul. "That girl is one in a million and so forgiving."

"That's true but there's something you need to know," Paul leaned forward. "I'm here to protect the woman I love."

"We don't understand."

"From here and going forward, if you want to have a relationship with Charlie then you're going to have to treat her right. You threw away a beautiful child and never gave her the chance to be all she should have been. But for the grace of God, that girl's life would have been destroyed and she would be dead. It's a marvel that she has so easily forgiven all of you and I won't put a damper on your reunion with Charlie. However, I'll be watching you closely to make sure that you never get the chance to hurt Charlie again."

"We've learnt our lesson," Mrs. Weston said, trying so hard to convince Paul of the fact. "What we did was so wrong, but from here and now, Charlie is a part of this family and we will treasure her." Something in Paul's eyes made her realise that he didn't believe her. "It's my promise that Charlie will never know another day of sorrow in this house again. I may not have acted as a mother should toward her but I'm ready to do that right now."

"That's good," Paul nodded. "I'm here to ask for her hand in marriage and will make her happy for the rest of her life."

"But we've only just found Charlie," her father protested mildly, turning red at the intense look in Paul's eyes.

"We won't go back into blaming or talking about the past. My family in Manchester is waiting to welcome Charlie and we are travelling back today because I intend to marry her as soon as possible. Please don't stand in the way of your daughter's happiness again. She deserves to be free and happy, so you need to let her go."

"We won't ever stand in the way of our daughter's happiness, but we need some time with Charlie."

"Well Mr. Weston, we have to ask Charlie herself, and whatever she decides is what we'll abide by."

Of course, once Charlie found out that Paul was ready to marry her, she opted to go with him at once. "Papa, Mama, I know that you want me to stay here, but I have to go back with Paul because that's where my life is," she smiled sweetly at them. "But rest assured that whenever I find the time, I will always come and visit you. But I have to travel to Manchester because that's where we both work."

"Oh and another thing," Paul smiled at Charlie and she saw the love in his eyes. "My surname is actually Baden. Vermont is my mother's father's name and also my middle name." At first Charlie didn't grasp his meaning. But then light slowly dawned on her and her eyes widened.

"Baden as in Baden Textiles?" Paul nodded. "But how didn't people know who you were?"

"Because I haven't always lived in Manchester. My elder brother had been running the factory with my father until he got married. His wife is a nice woman but very frail and she's been very ill. The weather wasn't fine for her, and he has had to move to the South of

France where we have another factory. The weather there is better for my sister-in-law, and so my father asked me to return home and take over. But I didn't want people to pretend that they were working hard just because they knew who I was. That was the reason I opted to come in as a loader and packer, someone of lowly means and of no consequence. Also, I was looking for a godly woman to marry and my heart settled on you, Charlie. But you had so much pain and the only way to help you was to ask you to come back here and make peace with your family. And now that you have done so, there's nothing stopping me," and he pulled out the ring he'd carried for a while now, and everyone gasped. It was so beautiful, a single diamond on a gold ring. "Charlotte Weston, before your whole family, will you be my wife?"

"Yes," Charlie was laughing and crying at the same time. "Yes, and yes over and over again."

"This is Charlie, the woman I love," Paul pulled her forward, and Charlie felt quite shy at the ten or so people in the large living room. If Charlie had thought her father was prosperous, she was stunned at Paul's family and just how wealthy they were. Their house was a small castle and as he was showing her round, he'd told her that it had belonged to a distant relative who had been a baron or something.

"We're not nobles, just gentry," he explained. "I know that there's a title on my mother's side but who cares about that? The important thing is that we are a happy family."

And now as Charlie met Paul's parents and his siblings and their spouses, she finally felt like she belonged somewhere. While she was happy she had made peace with her own family, it would take a bit of time for her to really open up to them. But she had promised as they were leaving that they would be invited for the wedding. It was still Christmas Day and she knew that she would never forget this day. On this day, she had finally found peace and acceptance.

"Brethren, I count not myself to have apprehended; but this one thing I do, forgetting those things which are behind, and reaching forth unto those things which are before." It wasn't going to be easy to completely forget the past because she had lived with so much pain for eighteen years, which was her whole life. But with the help of the loving man who had believed in her and refused to let her give up, she knew she would make it. Yes, she would reach forward for the things that the Lord had prepared for her to enjoy which included a loving husband and children one day.

"She is so beautiful, Paul," his mother came forward with outstretched arms. She had such a warm smile that Charlie nearly burst into tears when she took her in her arms for a hug. It was such a loving and maternal hug, something she'd never once experienced in her life and she knew that she was finally home.

One by one, Paul's siblings shook her hand or hugged her and made her feel so welcome. This was the family she had longed for, and as she recalled her childhood dream, she smiled. Yes, her Heavenly Father had come down and taken her away from all her pain, brought her into a beautiful home which was hers for the rest of her life, and given her a new name and family.

After so many years of pain and shame, she had finally received a very special Christmas Benediction, that of being loved by a good man and accepted wholly by his family.

FORGIVING EVERYTHING

ear Papa,

"**D**This is your daughter Charlotte or Charlie as everyone took to calling me all my life. Now I can finally say thank you for bringing me into this world and really mean it with a clean heart, unlike before when I was very bitter at the part you played in giving me life. Papa, I have lived a very hard life and been filled with so much bitterness because of the way I was treated in your house. For many years I planned how I would one day get vengeance against you and the whole family. But not anymore! I am a new creature now because of the *love of Jesus Christ in my heart. As He forgave me, so do I forgive everything and everyone who ever wronged me.*

If I don't pour my heart out, then this letter won't fulfil its purpose. I was only ten years old when I found out why my mother, who is really my stepmother, hated me so much. I was in your study on that day when you and Mama were arguing about me and heard everything that was said. It broke my heart to know that I was an unwanted child right from conception. Papa, when you forced yourself on my poor innocent mother, she was only a child, fourteen years old. You didn't protect her after that, and her life was so hard that she died three days after giving birth to me. Even after my mother's death, you rejected me, and I was treated worse than a servant in your own home.

All the beatings, the humiliation, the anger directed toward me when all I wanted was to be treated like my siblings nearly broke my heart. But I held on to hope, as young as I was, believing that one day your heart would change toward me and you would show me love. But that was until the day that you threw me away.

Papa, life in the workhouse was hell. When people are happy and living well, they say there's heaven on earth. Well, I would also like to tell you that there is hell on earth and that is to be found in the place called the workhouse. God preserved my life and virtue so many times, Papa, or else I might have ended up like my mother, pregnant at a very young age and abandoned by everyone. Or maybe even dead of a broken body and a shattered heart.

Now that I have gotten that off my chest, I want to say that I'm very sorry because I wasn't the daughter you wanted or deserved. Behold, as King David said, I was conceived in sin, and because of that, your marriage to my stepmother was really strained. Please forgive me for the part I played in causing you both so much unhappiness. Forgive me and forgive my dead mother so that I will finally have peace. I like to believe that she found peace from all her pain upon her death.

And I also choose to forgive every wrong thing that was done to me while I was in your house and even after. I forgive you for rejecting and throwing me away. Now I realise that the Lord was working all things for my good, after all. It is because of my time in the workhouse that I managed to become the person that I am today; strong and fearless. And everything that happened led me to the arms of a wonderful man who wants to marry me.

His name is Paul Vermont and he is a loader at the textile factory where I work. It is because of him that my heart finally opened up and I decided to come and make my peace with you all.

By the time you get this letter, I'll be back in Manchester. I don't know if we'll ever meet on this side of heaven but I'm hoping that one day your heart will become tender toward me.

As I sign off, I want to tell you that I love you. I wish I could have seen you and told you all this face to face. But since you're in London and I'm going back to Manchester, this isn't possible.

With all of the love of your eldest child,

Charlie."

"Dear Mama,

I know that you are my stepmother and I thank you for tolerating me for the first ten years of my life. It wasn't easy for you and I now realise that because I'm in love with a man who has promised to love and cherish me all the days of his life. I'm sure that my father promised you the same thing but then he betrayed your love and with a chambermaid no less.

Mama, I beg for your forgiveness on behalf of my father and my dead mother too. What they did was so wrong, and I ask you to forgive them. Be happy with my father and put all your pain behind.

Mama, I also forgive you for all the pain you inflicted on me when I was in your house. You broke my fingers because I was playing the piano and you didn't like it. Mama, I won't ask why you did that because this letter is all about forgiveness and restitution. I forgive you for all the humiliation, calling me names that I never deserved and compelling my father to throw me away and put me in a workhouse.

We can't revisit the past to change it because whatever happened, happened. However, I am choosing to remove every grudge and bitterness toward you from my heart. Maybe we shall one day meet and even if we don't, just know that I bear you no ill.

Thank you once again.

With love,

Charlie, your stepdaughter."

"Dear Chelsea,

My almost twin sister. While we were growing up it never once occurred to me that we weren't the children of the same mother. I loved you and wanted to be your older twin sister.

Please forgive me because my presence in the family denied you the chance to be Papa's eldest *child. It wasn't my fault that I was born, and I hope that you will remove every bitterness toward me.*

Chelsea, all the terrible things you did to me so that I would be hurt and humiliated are forgiven. Life has been very painful for me and I just pray that you'll never have to go through what I did. Still, there's always light at the end of the tunnel and right now I am at peace.

We may never meet on this side of heaven, but I love you.

Your older sister by two weeks,

Charlie."

"Dear Tiffany,

My sweet little sister! I really wanted to be the kind of older sister that you looked up to, told your secrets to and shared everything with. It was painful that we were never allowed to develop such a relationship.

But I won't blame you for anything since we were all children and didn't know better. However, please forgive me for not being the older sister you deserved. My presence in your life brought you the kind of pain that made you lash out to hurt me. All that is forgiven, and I wish you well in all your life.

I love you,

Charlie."

"Dear Albert,

My lovely brother, I hope you have grown up into a responsible young man now after eight years of not seeing you.

Al, please forgive me for not being the older sister you deserved. It wasn't anyone's fault but that's just how life was supposed to be, I guess. It's no use writing you a long letter because I know that many of the things you did were out of childish ignorance.

Nevertheless, I must extend the grace of forgiveness to you, too.

I love you,

Charlie."

"Dear Will,

This is one of the shortest letters that I have ever written but it needs to be done. You're a lovely brother and I hope you are becoming a responsible teenager now. I haven't seen you in eight years and I miss you. You must be quite tall now, if you took after our father.

Will, please forgive me for not being the older sister that you deserved. And I forgive you for everything that was wrong between us. It would have been wonderful to have a good relationship with you, but that is life anyway.

I love you,

Charlie."

"*Little Brother Trevor,*

You were still small when I left home, about five years old or so and you might not remember me well. But I remember you and the day you were born. Mama and Papa were so happy and so was I.

Sadly, we never got the chance to have a relationship like brother and sister. Whatever happened in the past is forgiven and one day all that will just be a distant memory. I also forgive you as I ask for your forgiveness for not being the sister you deserved.

Till we meet one day,

I love you,

Charlie."

It took a long time for all the crying and sobbing to die down in the Weston household when everyone had read the letters that Charlie had left them. What saddened them at the time was that she was long gone back to

Manchester with her fiancé and so they couldn't face her to beg for her forgiveness once more. After Paul had asked for her hand in marriage and they had received Mr. Weston's blessing, they had immediately left for the train station.

"There's hope," Mr. Weston told his wife when they were in their bedchamber later that night. "It feels so good to have received Charlie's forgiveness."

"That child is so special, and it will forever haunt me that I never realised that until it was too late."

"She is a good child and one day I know things will be well between us."

EPILOGUE

O ne Year Later

"My sisters want to come and visit us," Charlie told her husband as he was soothing their three-week-old son to sleep. "I sent my parents a message that I had put to bed and then Chelsea and Tiffany wrote to me asking if they could come and help with the baby. What do you think?"

Paul smiled at his wife. He would give her anything she wanted but her family visiting wasn't something he wanted, at least not right now when she was still weak from the ordeal of childbirth. He knew that her sisters were envious of her good life and he didn't trust them, not one bit. True, they were trying to be nice and he'd read a few of the letters they had exchanged with Charlie over the months. But it was his duty to protect his sweet wife who was so forgiving and saw only good in everyone.

The change in Charlie for the past one year had been remarkable. From a cold and bitter woman, she was now so sweet and gentle and loving. And it would be very easy for her sisters to take advantage of her if he didn't look out for her.

"Paul?'

"It's good of them to want to visit but you've only recently put to bed and need all the rest you can get. I understand that you want your family with you, but the baby is also still very small and right now we should defer the visit until a later date. Between my mother, sisters and sister-in-law as well as the servants and even cousins and aunts, we have more than enough people to help with the baby."

Charlie felt great relief at her husband's words. While she was mending the bridges with her family, she still didn't feel so comfortable having them around her all the time. They had come for her wedding a year ago and she'd been slightly stressed at the way Chelsea and Tiffany had tried to show her up. Thankfully, Paul's mother was a no-nonsense woman who had soon put them in their place. And over the months as they had been exchanging letters, she realised that they envied her, and she was still vulnerable.

"I will write and ask them to come next Christmas," she said.

"My love, you need all the rest you can get. I'll send them letters so that I can also enclose some cash gifts for all of them. Don't worry yourself about it."

"Thank you."

Paul smiled at his sleepy wife. "You go to sleep now, and I'll be back later when you've woken up again."

He had no intention of promising the two girls anything. He would write and tell them that this wasn't a good time to visit without committing himself in any way. In fact, he would keep deferring their visits until Charlie was strong enough both emotionally and physically to stand up for herself.

This was his wife's life and happiness, and she deserved rest and wellness more than anything.

And for the rest of her life, Charlie knew that her husband loved her deeply. Their love for each other grew stronger day by day, and she appreciated him for protecting her all the time. Eventually her sisters met men and got married and they maintained a relationship of some sort, but Paul always made sure that no one ever took advantage of his beautiful wife again.

And they lived a long and happy life together.

THANK YOU FOR CHOOSING A
PUREREAD BOOK!

We hope you enjoyed the story, and as a way
to thank you for choosing PureRead we'd like
to send you this free book, and other fun
reader rewards…

Click here for your free copy of Whitechapel
Waif
PureRead.com/victorian

AND THERE'S MORE...

We also want to bless you with a first chapter
of Rosie Swan's brand new Christmas
Victorian Romance, Workhouse Girl's
Christmas Dream.

Turn the page and let's begin...

WORKHOUSE GIRL'S CHRISTMAS DREAM

PART 1 - CHRISTMAS STORMS

C hristmas Day, Walsall County, England.

The storm that had been threatening for days reached the mining village of Walsall when least expected. Its violence was particularly felt in the old farmhouse that stood next to the village crossroads early in the morning on Christmas Day. A clap of thunder as loud as a blast from the dynamite used in the coal miles rumbled across the house, shaking its very foundations. A bolt of lightning sliced through the sky and struck a tree out in the yard, which immediately burst into flames. It seemed as if nature itself were sending out an ominous sign to the inhabitants of the old farmhouse that morning.

The flaming tree frightened the little girl whose face was pressed to the window as she watched nature in all her glory. She jumped back and crouched under the window sill like a scared rabbit, her eyes wide and filled with terror. In her whole life she'd never seen something as fascinating or as frightening as lightning striking a tree and causing it to burst into flames. That was the tree that she and her parents liked to sit under in the summer, sipping lemonade and watching as the villagers went past. Once in a while villagers would stop and be offered a glass of lemonade to refresh their thirsty throats. Now there would be no more reposing under the tree, and smoke from the burning tree filled the house, causing the child to choke.

For many years to come, eleven-year-old Amanda Jane Wood would always associate Christmas Day with terrible storms, fire, smoke and fear. First, fear of the terrible storm that was raging outside and then also the dark shadow of death that hovered in the three-roomed farmhouse. She coughed and tried to cover her face but in vain; the smoke was thick in the small living room.

Rain blew into the house through one of the cracked windows, soaking the child as she cowered under the windowsill. She rushed out of the living room and went to find her mother who was in her bedchamber. Mandy knew that when her parents' door was closed she wasn't supposed to open it without knocking first. And even then, she had to wait until she was bid to enter, so she stood there with her small hand raised as she prepared to knock. The storm made it impossible for her to hear whatever was going on and she knocked softly then waited.

Mrs. Edna Wood had just finished giving her husband a bed bath and dressing him in his best clothes as a way of preparing him for what was to come. Husband and wife both knew that this day wasn't going to end happily as most Christmas Days in the past had. That was the reason the twenty-nine-year-old man had held onto his wife's hand for a long while. The storm raged on outside, but in this small cosy room two souls were bidding farewell to each other, even though neither wanted to let go.

"Promise me that you'll always take care of Mandy," he whispered, his voice raspy even as his chest heaved. He was struggling to breathe, and she wished he would reserve his strength because talking was taking its toll on him. His once-ruddy skin was now sallow, and she could see the veins on his scrawny hands. Her once-virile man, the champion of her heart, was now nothing but skin and bones. Her heart was breaking, but she put on a brave smile. "And promise me that you'll also take good care of yourself."

"I promise," her voice was also a whisper as she fought back her tears. She had wept in private for many days, and this wasn't the time to do it openly. She had to be strong even though all she wanted to do was raise her head and scream, and ask why this was happening to her happy family. Why did death have to come to one so young when there were many old people in the village, she asked silently, then repented for her wicked thoughts. God was the giver of life and He chose who to preserve and who to take away. It wasn't up to her to decide because she was just a mere human being. But it hurt to know that this was the last time she was going to be with this man who held her heart.

"And always tell her that I love her so much but I have to leave. It's time for me to go, even though I wish I could stay with her, with you, my darling." And his shaking hand brought her palm to his cracked lips where he placed a soft kiss. His face was lined with the fatigue that comes to one who has been ailing for a while and whose body is giving up the fight. "It was so good with you, Edna," he whispered as he let her hand drop, his own too weak to continue holding it, and he closed his eyes. He opened his eyes briefly and smiled, "If I had to do it again, I would choose you over every other woman in the world. I would love you and be with you; always remember that."

The woman nodded, and when he fell asleep, she gazed at the face of the man she had loved for nearly twelve years, and tears coursed down her cheek. Why was death so cruel? And what would happen to her and Mandy when her beloved was gone?

She wiped her eyes because she didn't want Mandy to see her tears and rose up to go and empty the small basin. That's when she met with Mandy at the door of the bedchamber and the child looked terrified.

"Mandy, what's frightened you like this?" She looked toward the living room which was filled with smoke. "And why is there so much smoke in the house? Have you been burning things again?" Her voice was unusually harsh; then she toned it down. "Mandy you know that I've always told you to be careful with fire."

"Mama, the tree in the yard is burning and then the rain is pouring into the living room," Amanda was shivering but whether from the cold or fear or both wasn't clear. "The lightning struck the tree and it started burning."

"I'll fix the window later," Edna wiped the sweat off her forehead with the corner of her sleeve.

"How is Papa? May I go in and see him now? He promised that he would tell me the Christmas story today, Mama."

Edna gave her daughter a sad smile, "Not now, Mandy," she whispered. "Papa is tired and resting." She was normally a strong woman but taking care of her sick husband for the past one month had taken its toll on her. Slender and of average height, her blue eyes were troubled as they settled on her only child. She didn't want to frighten Mandy, but things weren't looking good for them, and their future was uncertain. She knew that Mr. Wood wasn't going to make it to the evening, and she didn't want to imagine what would happen to them after today. He had been her rock from the moment they had met and she felt like she was falling with no one to hold her.

"Mama today is Christmas Day and Mrs. Fount said we should celebrate it at her house with them. Will we be going there later, and will Papa come with us?" Mandy asked as she followed her mother into the third room of the house which served as both kitchen and Mandy's bedroom. Her mother had partitioned the room with a curtain to separate the child's sleeping area from the side they prepared meals on.

"Indeed it's Christmas Day," Mrs. Wood responded absentmindedly as she stroked the fire in the grate. There was a pot of chicken bones on it from their dinner last evening. She was preparing some broth to feed her husband, even though he'd told her that he wasn't hungry any more.

Mandy looked around the kitchen and frowned slightly, wondering why her mother wasn't preparing the delicious pies that she always did when they were visiting their neighbours. In the past all the families in the village celebrated Christmas together and gathered at the home of anyone who chose to be the host for that particular year. This time it was Mrs. Fount who lived on the west side of them and whose house was much bigger than everyone else's in the village. Her husband was the village constable, and her two daughters Gillian and Alison, who were ten and eight respectively, were Mandy's best friends.

Christmas was always such a fun-filled and happy season, but Mandy had the strange feeling that it wasn't going to be like that this year.

"Ma?" Mandy saw the sadness on her mother's face.

"Yes my love?"

"You haven't baked anything to take to Mrs. Fount's house. Will we not have Christmas this year?"

Mrs. Wood sighed as she turned to her daughter. Now was the time for the truth which couldn't be hidden any longer.

"Mandy, you'll soon be twelve and are growing up, and I don't want to hide anything from you any longer."

Mandy felt fear but looked at her mother with wide eyes, hazel like her father's.

"You know that your father has been very ill this past one month and we were hoping he would get better. Sadly, that hasn't been the case, so all the money we had has been used up in getting him medicines. There's nothing left for me to buy even half a pound of ham to make pies, and we have no flour in the bin," She smiled and pulled Mandy close. "But I promise you that next year things will be better."

"So Papa will get better and then we'll have a good Christmas next year, Ma?"

"Oh Mandy," Edna had prayed for that miracle from the moment her husband had noticed the blood in his sputum when he coughed. That had been two months ago and she had done all she could, using all the traditional remedies she remembered her mother teaching her. From warm milk laced with honey, to boiled roots, there was nothing she hadn't tried. But the cough had only gotten worse and finally they had to accept the truth.

Mandy and her mother held each other for a while listening as the storm began to abate. As the storm died down, a heavy bout of coughing from the bedchamber made her mother immediately release her. She ran out of the kitchen.

Mandy wanted to follow her, but something held her back. She hated seeing her father suffering and especially when he tried to pretend he wasn't in pain. Her mother had told her that she shouldn't tire him by asking too many questions. She also didn't want to go back to the living room which was chilly and full of smoke. Her stomach rumbled with hunger and she wished her mother would serve her some of the broth that was bubbling merrily on the fire.

Mama would take care of things once she was done taking care of Papa, the child thought as she moved behind the curtain to her small cot. She climbed on it and curled up, feeling the warmth from her frayed blanket. Papa had promised to buy her a nice woollen one once he got better and she smiled at the thought.

Mandy never complained even when she went without a lot of the things that Jill and Ally possessed. She always believed that one day her father would buy her everything her heart desired, and so her life was filled with childish contentment.

Jill and Ally had a large bedroom in which they slept but Mandy loved her spot here in the kitchen. She always lay on her small bed and watched her mother cooking, most times falling asleep because of the warmth from the fire and having to be woken up to eat.

Her eyes felt heavy even as she listened to the murmuring voices in the other room. Her parents were probably talking about what to do for Christmas and she smiled as she closed her eyes. The little girl was soon asleep, unaware that life was about to change for them forever.

It was the wailing that roused Mandy from her deep sleep. At first she thought it was part of the dream she'd been having. But then she became aware of footsteps coming and going in the kitchen which had earlier been empty. And she could smell something besides the chicken broth that had been boiling on the fire. Pie and freshly baked bread!

The little girl's stomach growled again and she pushed the curtain aside and got off her narrow cot, wondering if her mother had been fibbing before. A smile broke out on her face as she saw the small kitchen table. It was loaded with many covered dishes emitting delicious aromas. Yes, Christmas Day was going to be a celebration and it was being held at their house.

"I must be dreaming," the child thought because just before she'd fallen asleep there had been nothing in the kitchen. Yet now the small table was groaning under the weight of all the dishes placed upon it. No one seemed to have noticed her yet so she reached out a hand to pick up a pie from the tray nearest to her bed. Mama wouldn't mind and besides, she was so hungry. She'd just taken the first bite out of the fruit pie when the loud wail came again and the small sweet pastry dropped from her hand to the floor.

"Mama," Mandy cried out, recognizing the wailing voice and rushing out of the kitchen, brushing past neighbours who moved out of the way for her. Her mother was in her bedchamber and Mrs. Fount and Mrs. Wiser another neighbour were seated on the bed on either side of her mother.

Mandy frowned because this room was her parents' private domain and she couldn't recall any time that neighbours had been allowed inside. And yet here they were and she couldn't see any signs of her father who was supposed to be in the bed that her mother and the neighbours were sitting on.

"Ma?" Mandy stood at the doorway, too scared to go into her parents' bedchamber. That her mother was crying and wailing clearly meant that something bad had happened. The only other time she'd seen her mother this upset was years ago when she about four and her grandmother and grandfather had died just days apart from each other. And on that day Mandy had seen her father wrapping his arms around her mother and comforting her. But if something bad had happened, where was her father to comfort her mother again?

"Oh, Mandy," her mother caught sight of her and held her arms out. Mandy ran to her mother and fell into her arms. "Oh, Mandy," she repeated, tears clogging her throat.

Mandy suddenly got the feeling that she was never going to see her father again. At eleven years of age the young girl knew about death after losing both sets of grandparents when she was of an age of reasoning. And also, they lived in a mining village where they had one or two funerals a week. Though she was still too young to comprehend the effects of coal mining on the lives of the miners, she knew that people who worked in the mines were always dying; then they were buried and their families mourned.

When her grandparents had died, she and her mother had been comforted by her father. But he wasn't here now, and she'd never once thought that she would be one of those children in the village who lost their fathers. A few of her friends had buried their fathers, but Mandy always thought that such a misfortune was far from her. Now a red cord would be stuck to the front of their door, signifying that the angel of death had visited them, as her father liked to say.

"Papa?" She asked softly and her mother heard her. This had to be a bad dream and she willed herself to wake up.

"Mandy, we have to be strong. Your father has gone and left us," Mrs. Wood broke into sobbing even as her arms tightened around her daughter. "What will I do now without you, Anthony," the woman wailed.

"We're here for you and your daughter," Mrs. Fount put her arms around Mandy and her mother. "My family will help in every way that we can," she made the promise, which Mandy was to remember at a later date.

"Death comes to all of us at one time or other," Mrs. Wiser said, confirming Mandy's fears. Her father was dead and she knew that he would soon be put in a hole in the ground like all the other dead people she'd seen; they would cover him with earth and she would never see him again.

Then Mandy felt something rising within her, from her stomach it moved to her chest then throat and forced its way out of her in a wail that many would later say had sent chills down their backs.

"No," she struggled to get free of her mother's arms. Mrs. Fount's arms dropped but her mother's held fast. She wanted to be set free so she could go and meet her father at the end of the bridge where she liked to wait for him as he returned from the mines which were about two miles from the village. What her childish mind refused to accept was that the coal mines had claimed yet another victim, and this time it was her father. Anthony Wood, loving husband and beloved father was no more.

"Pa is coming back," the child wailed. "Let me alone so I can go and wait for him at the bridge," she struggled to get free but her mother's arms only tightened around her small body.

"Mandy, you have to be strong," Mrs. Wiser said. "Your mama needs you right now. Stop that nonsense at once and accept what has happened. Denying it won't make your father come back."

But the child ignored the woman's harsh rebuke and continued to struggle in her mother's arms. Finally Mrs. Wood's hands were too weak and tired to continue holding the struggling child and she let go. Mandy rushed out of the room, ignoring calls from the neighbours who seemed to be everywhere. Their small house was filled with people, but she brushed them all aside when they tried to reach for her. She raced through the small living room where she saw Mr. Fount, the police constable who also acted as coroner whenever anyone died, and she also saw Reverend Jones, the vicar of their parish along with a few other male neighbours. They were standing around talking, but she didn't wait to hear what they had to say.

"Mandy," another voice called out as she tore out of the house through the front door, noticing the red cord hanging from the door. Her eyes were fixed on the road. It had stopped raining and the sun was even trying to break through the thick clouds. Mandy's focus was on getting to the bridge where she would wait for her father and skip beside him all the way home. Usually he left a little bit of whatever her mother had packed for his lunch and gave it to her as a present for waiting for him.

Come rain or sunshine, the child never missed a day waiting for her father at the bridge, unless she was sick and in bed.

There were few people on the road on account of the heavy storm that had passed. And also, it was early afternoon on Christmas Day and most folks were at home taking long lunches or early dinners. But none of Mandy's friends whose fathers also worked in the mines were outside as usual. That didn't even occur to her as she ran on, even though she soon found herself alone on the road.

Usually all the children of Walsall Village whose fathers worked in the coal mines would race each other to Old Walsall Bridge and play there among the rocks until the men arrived. Then each child would walk or dance back home with their father.

Today, however, it didn't occur to Mandy that the road leading to the bridge was empty. Her grief seemed to her shrouded her in a world of her own, pushing her back into the past and she didn't even remember that it was Christmas Day and the mines were shut down until after the holidays. All she wanted was her father.

Mandy got to the bridge, crossed it and sat down on one of the many little rocks that someone had once called the waiting station. One or two people passed by, giving her odd looks but the child's eyes were fixed on the path that her father usually took from the mines.

"Not my Pa," Mandy muttered as a man hurried toward the bridge and crossed it to the other side. "Not my Pa," she said of yet another, getting into the game she and her friends usually played as they waited. The game would go on until one of the children spotted his or her father. Thereafter, the lucky child would jump up and shout,

"My Pa is here, no more delays, no more waiting," and the others would giggle and continue with the game until the last man had returned. Sometimes when there was an explosion or a cave in at the mines, the children and their mothers would huddle together at the 'waiting station', each praying that their father and husband wasn't the latest victim to be claimed by the mines.

"Mandy," the soft voice broke through the child's continuous muttering and she looked up to find her mother crossing the bridge.

"Ma," she said, "I've been waiting for my Pa, but he isn't here yet. And I haven't seen the other men returning. Are they still working in the mines?" Mandy's eyes returned to the path leading to the mines.

"Oh Mandy," her mother walked slowly towards her. Mandy noted that she looked very tired and her eyes were red. Mrs. Wood had suffered five miscarriages, and when she'd given up hope of ever having a child, Mandy had been conceived.

It was clear to all that the little girl was the apple of her parents' eyes, but rather than become pampered and spoiled, she had such a sweet nature that everyone in the village liked her. The traders and store owners always had little treats for her whenever her parents sent her to get groceries.

"Mandy, today is Christmas Day and the mines are closed for the holidays," her mother reminded gently. She sat down on the same rock as her daughter and stretched out her shawl to cover them both.

Mandy raised stricken eyes to her mother. "Then where is my Pa?"

"Oh, Mandy," Mrs. Wood pulled her daughter close. "It's so cold out here and I need to get you home where it's warm. Besides, we have visitors and shouldn't leave them alone or they will think that we're being very poor hosts."

"But Pa..."

"Mandy!" Her mother's voice was gentle but firm. "For the past one month your father never went to the mines and you know the reason why, don't you? Remember that you haven't been out here to the bridge in all that time," Mrs. Wood raised her daughter's chin. "Your Pa was very sick and he was hurting terribly. You even saw that sometimes he would cough out blood and then wasn't able to breathe properly. He wanted to stay with us but the pain was too much for him to bear," Mrs. Wood's voice broke on a sob. "He begged me to let him go even when I didn't want to, and told me to tell you that he loves you so much and will be watching over you from heaven."

"But he didn't ask me before he left," Mandy cried out. "Why didn't he ask me? I wouldn't have let him go."

"Mandy, your father didn't want you to be sad so he didn't ask you."

"Ma, but why did he leave us? Didn't he love us anymore?" Mandy began to sob. "Why did he find it so easy to leave us?"

"Mandy, he didn't find it easy to leave us because he held on for as long as he could," Mrs. Wood said. Her husband, like many other miners before him, had suffered from black lung disease, which had only worsened as the days went by. "Your Pa loved us both so much but the pain became unbearable, and I let him rest," Mrs. Wood sobbed. The two held each other close and wept together for a long while.

They sat there at the 'waiting station' until the village lamplighter passed over the bridge, his ladder in his hand, on his way to light the gas streetlights.

"We have to get back home," Mandy heard her mother saying as if from a distance. "It's getting dark and we don't want to be out here until late." She rose to her feet and pulled Mandy up. Mother and daughter walked back home hand in hand, stopping every few steps to receive condolence messages from their neighbours.

And everyone had nice things to say about her father. Mandy heard them praising her father and saying that he was a good man who would be greatly missed. She wanted to shout and tell people not to talk about her father as if he wasn't there. Then she remembered that he was gone and actually wasn't there and fresh tears filled her eyes.

She would miss her Pa so much, and it was true: he'd been a very good man. Young as she was, Mandy understood what love was because she'd seen and experienced it in her home. And her father never stopped telling her and her mother that he loved them with his whole heart. Though they didn't have much, no one in need was ever turned away from their door.

"Even if there's nothing to eat in the house, make sure that everyone who comes to our door gets at least a simple glass of water," were her father's words to her so many times.

Mandy never understood why her father was so generous, sometimes causing her mother to complain that he was too kind. But Mr. Wood would simply laugh, ruffle Mandy's hair and kiss his wife's cheek.

"The Apostle Paul tells us to always open our homes to strangers for who knows, we may one day even welcome an angel into our humble abode," he would say. "And always remember that…"

"Angels are messengers who bring blessings from God to His people," Mandy and her mother would finish his sentence and they would all laugh.

It was because of her father's example that Mandy had learned to share everything she had with her friends. But sometimes they weren't as giving as she was, and she would then get upset and complain to her father.

"Mandy, don't always expect to be repaid for your kindness and generosity," he'd once told her when Jill and Ally refused to share their pastries with her. She had complained to him that her friends were very mean and yet she always shared everything with them. "Just do good, and one day it will find you when you need it most. God always rewards generosity even if it isn't immediately. What you hand out to someone through the front door returns to you through the back door."

Mrs. Wood paused at their small gate and Mandy looked up to see that someone had already lit the lanterns in the house and even placed two on the small porch. Their house was brighter than usual and she could see the red cord hanging on the open door. She wanted to rush up and tear it down.

Their small living room was filled with people and as soon as Mandy and her mother entered the house, the mourners parted to let them through. And that was when Mandy saw her father lying on the bier, covered up to his neck with a white sheet. He looked so peaceful and it was as if his lips were about to burst into a smile like they always did. Her Pa was such a happy man and she couldn't remember ever seeing him sad.

There was silence in the house as everyone watched to see what the child would do. They had seen her running out before and were worried that she wasn't in a very good frame of mind.

Mandy approached the bier, "My Pa looks like he's sleeping," she spoke to no one in particular. Mr. Anthony Wood looked peaceful in death, just as he had in life. "I wish he would open his eyes and wake up," she murmured.

She stood beside the bier for a long time, not feeling afraid of the dead body as was her usual practice. Even when a neighbour died and her parents took her to pay their respects to the family, Mandy would never get close to the bier.

Yet now she drew close without any fear, putting out a hand to touch her father's cold face. "Pa is cold," Mandy said, adjusting the bed sheet. A sob broke out among the mourners but Mandy ignored it. "I wish he was still here with us," she said sadly.

Then she turned to find her mother watching her. So she walked to where she was and put her arms around her.

"Ma, please don't ever go away like Pa and leave me alone."

Mrs. Wood choked up, "Oh, Mandy!"

"Now what will we do without my Pa," the child asked in a soft voice, sounding very lost.

What will happen to Mandy and her mother?

Workhouse Girl's Christmas Dream is a heartbreakingly beautiful Christmas story of rags to riches set in Victorian England. Mandy's story is one you will enjoy to the final happy ever after…

Continue Reading on Amazon

Continue Reading on Amazon

LOVE VICTORIAN ROMANCE?

If you enjoyed this story why not continue straight away with other books in our PureRead Victorian Romance library?

Read them all...

Orphan Christmas Miracle

An Orphan's Escape

The Lowly Maiden's Loyalty

Ruby of the Slums

The Dancing Orphan's Second Chance

Cotton Girl Orphan & The Stolen Man

Victorian Slum Girl's Dream

The Lost Orphan of Cheapside

Dora's Workhouse Child

Saltwick River Orphan

Workhouse Girl and The Veiled Lady

OUR GIFT TO YOU

AS A WAY TO SAY THANK YOU WE WOULD LOVE TO SEND YOU THIS BEAUTIFUL STORY FREE OF CHARGE.

Our Reader List is 100% FREE

Click here for your free copy of Whitechapel Waif

PureRead.com/victorian

At PureRead we publish books you can trust. Great tales without smut or swearing, but with all of the mystery and romance you expect from a great story.

Be the first to know when we release new books, take part in our fun competitions, and get surprise free books in your inbox by signing up to our Reader list.

As a thank you you'll receive an exclusive copy of Whitechapel Waif - a beautiful book available only to our subscribers...

Click here for your free copy of Whitechapel Waif

PureRead.com/victorian

Printed in Great Britain
by Amazon

21273929R00135